I0623161

ABOUT THIS BOOK

After her brush with death, a young girl's humanity is at risk, and a guardian angel must choose between loving her and protecting her. Sequel to *Avenoir*.

Heidi Bennett's destiny was changed forever on the night of the Cold Moon Ball two winters ago. Months later, she was given a second chance at life—one that was supposed to restore life back to normal. Unfortunately for Heidi, things are not that simple.

The angels who know exactly what happened to her don't quite understand what she has become. Being able to read people's memories and learn secrets of many residents in Havenwood Falls is just one of the consequences. As time passes, Heidi distances herself more and more from the human she used to be, testing the boundaries of her new abilities. But when she's manipulated by a mysterious entity that controls her dreams, her behavior goes from reckless to downright dangerous.

With a desire to restore her humanity, guardian angel Zane becomes involved. Torn between his responsibilities as an angel and his love for Heidi, Zane has to decide between the two—but can he protect her if he turns his back on his own kind?

HAVENWOOD FALLS HIGH BOOKS

Predestined by Valia Lind

Rediscovered by Morgan Wylie

Ashes of Fate by Apryl Baker

Stay up to date at www.HavenwoodFalls.com

ALSO BY DANIELE LANZAROTTA

Academy of the Fallen Series – YA

Wide Awake

Nephilim

Sins of the Fallen

Forsaken

Sudden Hope Novels – YA

Sudden Hope

Catch Me If I Fall

Imprinted Souls Series – YA

Imprinted Souls

Bloodlust

Divine Ashes

Blood Bound

Shattered Souls

Reawakening Series – YA

Venom

Blood Ties (Coming 2019)

A Mermaid's Curse Trilogy – Adult

Insatiable

Fated

Unbreakable

Individual Titles

The Right Kind of Wrong – Adult

Lost Souls – YA

The Sinners – Adult

BLURRED LINES

A HAVENWOOD FALLS HIGH NOVELLA

DANIELE LANZAROTTA

Copyright © 2019 Daniele Lanzarotta, Ang'dora Productions, LLC

All rights reserved.

Published by

Ang'dora Productions, LLC

5621 Strand Blvd, Ste 210

Naples, FL 34110

Havenwood Falls and Ang'dora Productions and their associated logos are trademarks and/or registered trademarks of Ang'dora Productions, LLC.

Cover design by Regina Wamba at reginawamba.com

Except as permitted under the U.S. Copyright Act of 1976, no part of this publication may be reproduced, stored in a retrieval system, or transmitted in any form or by any means, electronic, mechanical, photocopying, recording, or otherwise, without written permission of the owner of this book.

Please do not participate in or encourage piracy of copyrighted materials in violation of the author's rights. Purchase only authorized editions.

This book is a work of fiction. Names, characters, and events are either products of the author's imagination or are used fictitiously, and any resemblance to actual persons, living or dead, is entirely coincidental.

To the readers who fell in love with Heidi and Zane.

CHAPTER 1

ZANE

I sit on the roof at the house across the street from Heidi's and stare at her window from a distance. I've been sitting here for hours, and the open window has become this cruel joke. I can't stand knowing that she's right there, yet that I must stay away. Her lights are out, and the music is blasting. As much as I hate to admit it, I miss the pop songs she used to listen to. At least those had lyrics that could be understood. These new songs that she seems to like now sound like someone is screaming incoherently at you.

"Well, well." I hear a female's voice from behind me. I turn around to find Gabriella wearing a blue dress and high-heeled boots. She annoyingly taps her foot on the roof. Her arms are crossed, but she smiles when my eyes meet hers. "It's about time you decided to listen to me and check in on your girl. And thank you for clearing the snow off the roof this time."

I glare at Gabriella, the angel who has been keeping an eye on Heidi while I serve my punishment for bringing her back to life.

"She is not my girl," I say in a cold tone, to hide the fact that I wish more than anything that she could be.

Gabriella gives me a dramatic eye roll, then extends her hand.

1

"I need your jacket," she says. I take off my leather jacket and hand it to her. She lays it down and sits on top of it.

"Seriously?" I ask.

She shrugs. "It's not like you really need it. And I'd hate for my dress to get dirty."

"Yeah, because that seems like something you should be worried about," I say.

"Watch your tone, angel," she says jokingly. "I'm over here helping you out of the goodness of my heart, when I really shouldn't. You asked for help, and I volunteered to be her guardian angel, but I should be reporting all the stupid little things she has been pulling. Yet I'm keeping them a secret."

I look away and sigh.

"How is she?" I ask.

She chuckles. "Do you mean since the last update I gave you just a few days ago? When I begged you to come?"

Growing impatient, I just shake my head. "It's not exactly easy for me to leave without them knowing. They think I'm watching over someone else right now." I pause. "Now can you please just stop torturing me and answer the question?" I beg.

"Such a funny request coming from someone who is known to be incapable of giving straight answers," she says in a sarcastic tone.

I glare at her.

Gabriella puts her hands up. "Fine . . . fine. She's not doing any better. She's not herself. She's lonely. She skips school. She wanders around in the woods. The list goes on and on . . . and there is not much I can do without breaking rules to intervene with her life."

I sigh. I used to hate watching Heidi and Jace together. Since they have broken up, I hate the fact that she's alone even more. At least he was good for her. He was helping her heal in ways I cannot.

"I'm sure she's just acting out," I say. "She and Jace aren't together. I'm certain she's just sad, depressed—whatever human reaction is normal in those cases. She'll come around."

"Argh." Gabriella lets out a frustrated growl. "And that is exactly why I begged you to come back—so you can see it for yourself."

I open my mouth to argue with her, but she cuts me off.

"And yes, she is lonely. She barely talks to anyone, but that and her other behaviors can't possibly be for breaking up with someone she fell out of love with."

I lean my head down. "How do you know she fell out of love with him?"

Gabriella pauses, but I keep my head down. I'm afraid to hear her answer out loud.

"You know," she says, "for someone who has been around for so many decades, you sure are dense." Her tone grows frustrated.

I look up and stare at Heidi's window again.

"She's not home, by the way," she finally says.

"Where is she? Why aren't you watching her?" I growl.

She chuckles. "Let's say she has become an expert at escaping." She nods toward the window. "The lights out and music thing seems mostly to fool her parents. They think she's sleeping. I followed her all the way to her dad's market on Miller's Plaza. She probably knew I was near. She left through the back door without me noticing. We both know we lost the ability to track her, so I decided to just come straight here and wait."

I stand up, agitated, and start to pace back and forth on the roof. "Any idea where we should look? Where has she been going lately?"

She shrugs. "You could go to the library and look for her. I know she liked spending time there. Or you can sit and wait. She'll come back home eventually. She always does."

CHAPTER 2

HEIDI

I sit at the dinner table, staring at my plate as Mom lectures me about missing school. This is our new routine. As Mom goes on and on about being disappointed, Dad gets lost in a memory of us eating a peaceful dinner together just a little over a year ago. I was excitedly telling them about my day at school and then about my dance recital's costume. He misses how things used to be. I know that, logically, I should too. But I feel nothing.

That was before I was killed. December 2, 2018, was the night I disappeared. Hurt by some screwed up angel, I ended up in a coma and died months later. Another angel, Zane, brought me back to life, and somehow, I came back with a special ability to read people's memories. If Mom and Dad only knew . . . Like most, they believe I have no recollection of what really happened to me. They just know that I went missing and eventually found my way back. I wonder if things would be less awful for them if they knew that this curse to pick up on people's memories is what destroyed so many things I used to love. I can see every single detail of a memory with such clarity, it is as if I were there at the moment when it happened. Some days—well, most days—I just need a break.

"I'm going to bed," I tell Mom in the middle of her sentence. She just sighs and throws her napkin down on the table. I can tell she's on the verge of giving up on me. I can't believe she hasn't already.

Without looking back, I rush upstairs and slam my door shut. I turn the music on and pace back and forth. This music tends to numb my thoughts in a way, but tonight, nothing seems to be helping. I feel like I'm all over the place. I feel irritable about . . . well, everything.

"I need to get out of here," I say out loud.

I put on a dark hoodie and coat and walk out of my room, locking the door from the inside and putting a hair clip in my pocket so I can get back in later. If Mom and Dad come to check on me, they'll think I'm doing homework or that I fell asleep. I quietly make my way downstairs. I hear them talking in the kitchen, so I go the other way, grabbing Dad's store keys on the way out.

I curse myself for not waiting until later to leave. I have come to love nighttime, when there is barely anyone out. Right now, the streets have more people than I care to see. I avoid going anywhere near Town Square to get to Miller's Plaza, but even the back roads have a few tourists walking around and admiring the small-town charm and stunning mountain views. I roll my eyes at the sound of that. You'd think after a day of skiing, they would be tired and want to lock themselves in their rooms.

I freeze in place when I see a family of four walking around. The parents carry the two little boys. Based on their memories, I can tell they are visiting from Italy. *If they only knew they're putting their kids in danger just by walking around at night*, I think to myself. Anger consumes me as I start to wonder how many of these tourists will actually make it back home after vising here.

I decide to approach the couple.

"Excuse me," I say. The young couple stops walking and looks at me with smiles on their faces, even though they look tired.

There is no telling how long they've been walking around carrying their kids in the snow.

"Hello," they say.

I smile back. There is no easy way to tell them this. I look at my watch. "Are you heading back to where you are staying? It's not too safe to be out at this time of night."

Well, that didn't sound creepy at all.

"But you are out," the man says in a heavy accent.

I take a deep breath and try not to sound rude. "Well, yes, but I live right here," I tell them. "And I know what I am talking about. It's not safe."

Yep. They think I'm crazy. I can tell by the nonchalant look in their eyes.

"Thank you," they say and start to walk again.

I sigh. It's not like they would have believed me if I told them there are vampires roaming around—among other things.

I keep walking west, and once I get to Miller's Plaza, I absentmindedly stop in front of the dance studio I used to love. I zone out for a while. It's the feeling of my fingernails digging into my skin that brings me back to the here and now. I turn around and keep walking toward my dad's market.

Once in the market, I welcome the quiet of being here after hours—when the store is free of people walking around. Thankful for Dad being in the midst of switching security systems, I take my time walking down every aisle, even though I know what I'm here for. When I get to the aisle with hair products, I stop and stare at the variety of options. I grab the darkest one I can find. *Perfect.* I need a change, and this is fitting. I make my way to the back of the store. Dad bought a machine to make T-shirt designs shortly after he bought the store, so he can make some extra cash during the many town events and fundraisers. From that day, I started to design my own collection of shirts. I grin at the thought of people's reactions when I start wearing them.

As the first one is printing, I grab a bag of chips and a can of soda from the office. I sit down and reach for the can first.

"Ouch." I feel the small piece of metal piercing through my skin as I open the can. It's a small scratch, but enough to cut through my skin. I watch it as it quickly heals right before my eyes. This happened once before with a paper cut, and it healed just as fast. I stare at my finger for long after it is healed. *Maybe I should be happy about this.* I chuckle. *Happy—I can't even remember what that feels like.* Either way, this just opens up a whole new set of questions—like what the hell am I? I see my parents' memories. They miss the cheerful, sweet, nice daughter I once was. Not the distant, alone, cold version of her that they have today.

"Ugh. Snap out of it, Heidi," I tell myself. I open the bag of chips and start eating it.

I spend the next half hour or so enjoying my peace and quiet, until I get a text from Ani Rukska, the witch who made it possible that I no longer pick up on Jace's memories, and the only person whom I've told the truth about my abilities.

Ani: I'm by the back door of the store. We need to talk.

I roll my eyes and contemplate just ignoring her message, but unfortunately, that doesn't mean she will go away.

I hop off the office chair and let her in.

She closes the door behind her, and I cross my arms over my chest.

"How did you know I was here after hours?" I ask.

She grins. "Location spell," she says proudly. She pauses. "By the way, someone followed you here."

Of course, I think to myself. That is the angel Zane has following me around. I can't pick up on her memories to know when she's around, but luckily, she doesn't care to hide the fact that I'm being watched.

"I'm aware," I say. "Female, long hair, dark skin, extremely well dressed?" I ask in an annoyed tone.

"Yep. That would be the one."

"So . . . Do you want to go somewhere else and talk?" I ask.

She nods. "That would be best. Let's go to my house."

"Just give me a few minutes," I say. I turn off the machine and grab the first few shirts and the bag with hair dye. I throw the drink and bag of chips out, but leave the lights on so the angel thinks I'm still here. Dad will probably just think that he forgot to turn it off anyway. We get out through the back door, and I follow Ani to her house.

When we are some distance away from the store, she chuckles.

"What?" I ask.

"I'm guessing you escaped from her before?" she asks.

I shrug. "Wouldn't you have? I don't particularly like being followed." I pause. "Or found through location spells," I snap.

She smirks. "Something is different about you. Sneaking out, being out this late, snappy comments," she says. "I like it."

I roll my eyes at her. "I'm sure you do."

We continue the walk in silence. At some point, I hear howling in the distance, but those sounds don't even faze me anymore. I find it amusing that Ani watches me to see if I react at all. She doesn't say anything when she realizes that I don't. When we get to her house, I walk in after her.

A part of me expected to walk in and find potions and such all over the place, but her house is actually normal. No one would even be able to tell that she is what she is.

"So, what is it that you wanted to talk about?" I ask.

"Have a seat," she says. "Do you want something to drink?"

"I'm good. Thanks," I say in a cold tone. *Who in their right mind would accept a drink from a witch?*

"Okay, then," she says as she sits down. I remain standing. "I'll get right to it so you can get home. I'd like to collect on the favor you owe me."

"Go on," I tell her.

She hands me a piece of paper with five names. I read over them: Michaela Petran, Mathilde Augustine, Lilith Blackstone, Lawrence Mills, and Roman Bishop. I chuckle at the last name, as I already know a few of his secrets. I fold the list and look at Ani.

"I'd like to know everything you can get on their memories," she says.

I grin at her.

"Why would I do that?" I ask as I tilt my head to the side.

"Because you owe me," she says in an awkward tone.

I sigh. "Now, see . . . we have a difference in opinions about that. I came to you and asked you to keep me from reading memories in general and to forget a certain someone. All you did was block Jace's memories for me."

She stands up and closes the distance between us. She tries to look collected, but I can tell she's in shock. My grin widens.

"You're playing with fire, child."

"Am I?" I ask her.

She nods. Once. "I can just as easily undo that spell."

I shrug. "We have broken up since then. What's one more person's memories to pick up on?" I smile at her.

"I could tell your secret," she says.

I laugh. "You could. But then again, I have this list you just gave me. I'm sure you wouldn't want these people knowing of your interest in their memories—or that you knew about me and have been hiding my secret for your own selfish reasons."

She gapes.

I chuckle. "I guess I should let myself out," I say, turning around to leave.

"You don't know who you are messing with, little girl," she warns as I open the door.

"Uh huh," I say before heading home.

CHAPTER 3

ZANE

"*S*he wasn't at the library. Or at Jace's house," I tell Gabriella when I get back. She is calmly sitting on the roof, reading a fashion magazine. She slowly puts the magazine down on her lap, which drives me insane.

"Why would she be at Jace's?" she asks, confused.

I throw my hands up in the air. "I don't know! I didn't know where else to look! And why are you so calm?" I ask.

She smiles. "She got home not long ago. Listen." She pauses. "No music," she says. "I honestly don't think I could take another second of that."

I look toward the window, tempted to go in there and see her.

I try to make conversation with Gabriella to keep my mind off Heidi.

"What are you looking at?" I ask, sitting next to her.

"Just looking at dresses. The Sweetheart Dance is coming up. I was thinking about stopping by. You know . . . just to make sure Heidi stays on track."

"Why would she go to the dance?" I ask.

She shrugs, and I watch her as she flips through the pages. This is more than just about Heidi. Gabriella dresses up more than any angel I know.

"Any news on Bryson?" she asks, referring to the angel responsible for Heidi's death. I shake my head. "Nothing. Not that I've had much time to look, but as far as I know, no one has had any leads in a long time. It's like he vanished."

"Maybe you should give up on trying to find him. Spend any extra time you can get away here. Heidi needs you. I told you before—her behavior tends to improve slightly when you are around. I bet it would improve even more if you could actually stay a while."

I shake my head. "He could always try to come back and hurt her again. And your theory is nonsense," I tell her. "She's probably just acting out because she misses having someone. She misses Jace." I pause. "Is this your way of telling me you're getting tired of helping?" I ask.

She smiles. "On the contrary. Heidi keeps things interesting. Especially when she knows she's being followed. It has become a challenging game really. I haven't had this much action in decades."

"Keeping her safe is not a game," I growl.

Gabriella rolls her eyes at me.

"Do you actually think she will go?" I ask. "To the dance," I say when she gives me a puzzled look.

She nods. But something doesn't add up. She mentioned that Heidi likes to be alone. Why would she go to a dance? I don't bother asking or even trying to understand.

Gabriella goes back to looking through the magazine, while I sit here, looking toward Heidi's window.

When morning finally comes, Heidi doesn't come out when I expect her to.

"She should be at school by now," I tell Gabriella. "Did she look okay when she came back last night?"

She shrugs. "As far as I could see. I told you—skipping class seems to be her thing lately."

About thirty minutes go by before the front door starts to open.

"Hide," says Gabriella. We both go to the side of one of the two-story houses on her street and stand where she can't see us, since making myself invisible to humans no longer works with her.

The moment I see her, I'm stunned. Her hair is shorter and pitch black, contrasting with her light skin in a way that takes my breath away.

"Well, that is new," says Gabriella. "Edgy. I love it."

Gabriella goes on and on, but I stop listening at some point as Heidi consumes my full attention. I stand here and watch her walk away, heading toward the school, and I have to fight the urge I feel to go toward her.

Once she turns the corner, Gabriella pulls me back to reality. "Come on," she says. "I have things to show you."

I follow Gabriella to Heidi's room.

Her room looks the same as always, leading me to believe that Gabriella is exaggerating. At least that is what I think at first.

Gabriella grabs Heidi's laptop and opens it. "Here."

She hands it to me.

"It needs a password," I say.

She grins from ear to ear.

"Try your name." She laughs.

I look at her like she has gone mad.

"Do it," she orders. I do, and it works. I glare at her, warning her not to say a word about this.

On the screen, there is a story about a guy who is in love with two friends—dating one, dreaming about the other. I don't think much of it until I see their names . . . and last names.

"What's this?" I ask Gabriella.

"That, my friend, is a private blog where your girl writes every single memory she sees during the day."

I look down. "This is the only entry."

She smirks. "You're welcome," she says proudly. "Every day, I come here. I spend some time reading the material, and then I delete them."

"And she keeps writing them?"

She nods.

"Always in private?" I ask.

"Yes."

"Have you tried to delete the blog?"

"Once," she says. "She just started another. I figured I'd let her get it out of her system and then delete it." She pauses. "Besides," she continues, "it's quite amusing. The girl has a great future writing gossip columns if that is something she wants to pursue."

"Only, this is not gossip," I say. "If someone finds out . . ."

I shake my head, frustrated at how careless she has been. I decide to leave her a message on the computer. PLEASE STOP. I start to type my name under it but decide not to.

"What else has she been doing?" I ask, almost afraid of the answer.

"She's curious about things, Zane. I've seen her looking at certain people differently. Approaching people she didn't hang out with before, almost as if she is trying to pick up on their memories on purpose."

"Any idea on how we can fix this?" I ask.

She smiles. "There is a certain angel I know who is a great influence on her."

I lower my head. "I can't, Gabriella."

"Why not?" she asks. I don't answer her. As an angel, Gabriella has responsibilities of her own. I could never admit to her that I can't be near Heidi without wanting to be with her.

"I have my reasons," I tell her. "Just keep an eye on her for me, okay? I need to think, and I can't think straight here. I'll be back later." I say, and I leave, getting as far away from her room as possible—trying to escape from her scent—from every reminder of her.

CHAPTER 4

HEIDI

*W*alking to school, I can't help but to replay my talk with that witch. The look on her face . . . Standing up for myself like that felt great, and it was nice feeling something good for a change.

I take my time walking to school, knowing that I'm already going to be in trouble with Mom and Dad for being late anyway.

I stop at Coffee Haven on the way. I've been coming in here for years, but for the first time, I stop to look at the paintings and drawings by local artists displayed on the walls. I heard once that you can tell a lot by people's artwork—that sometimes, that is how they tell the world things they could never say out loud. So I stand here and analyze them, searching for anything supernatural. And I don't see anything out of the ordinary. Anger consumes me as I think about how the humans in town, including my parents and Jace, live every day under a threat they don't even know exists. I clench my fists. *I need to find a way to put an end to this,* I say to myself.

Feeling like I'm being watched, I turn toward the counter and fake a smile when I see Harlow Augustine looking at me curiously. She takes my order. I know she's wondering why I'm not in school, but I also pick up on memories of her telling someone how she feels bad for me going through so much—gone missing and then not remembering what happened, which is what everyone thinks. Like Ani, she is also a witch, but she doesn't rub me the wrong way. I also know I could never ask her for any favors or put her in a position where she needs to keep my secret, because she likely wouldn't. I knew that Ani lacked morals—Harlow, not so much. *Augustine.*

My mind goes back to the list, and curiosity piques again at why Ani would want information about them in particular. As I stand here waiting for my hot chocolate, I hope to pick up on any useful memories that Harlow may have of her grandmother, which was one of the names on the list.

Not getting anywhere, I finally ask her, "How is your grandma?" hoping that will at least trigger some thoughts.

Harlow just gives me a puzzled look. "She's good," she says, then turns around and hands me two hot chocolates with a smile on her face. I give her a confused look. She shrugs. "Give that to your teacher. Maybe he—or she—won't be too hard on you for being late."

I thank her and head to school, getting there during second period, in the middle of an English Lit pop quiz.

Mr. Zander looks up at me, and before he can say anything, I apologize for being late and hand him the drink.

"It's hot chocolate," I say in an apologetic tone.

"Take your seat, Ms. Bennett. Thank you for the drink, but you won't be getting any extra time to complete the quiz." I nod, turn around, and walk to my seat. I immediately curse myself for giving him the hot chocolate when I catch the curious look that Celeste and a few others give me. I have no doubt I'm being judged, and I wouldn't be surprised if someone starts spreading rumors that I hit on Mr. Zander. I know he is a popular bachelor and all, but . . . ew.

When lunch comes around, I don't go for my usual table, but I do sit alone. I usually grab a book from my bag and pretend to read, knowing that people are a lot less likely to bother me. But not today. Today, I sit next to a table with a few vampires and a shifter, among others. I put my lunch down on the table, then I pull my sweater over my head, showing off my black T-shirt that has the design of fangs. The writing on it says, *Vampires suck.* I can't even hide my grin as I sit here, even though I'm careful not to make direct eye contact with anyone in particular.

Soon, Miranda, who is one of them, sits at my table. I like Miranda, though. She's always been nice, and there is something about her cheerful personality that draws people in—even me. She laughs. "Nice shirt. Where did you get it?"

I tell her I ordered it online. The last thing I want is to get my dad in trouble, or put him in danger. After I say that, the conversation goes dead, which is not normal when Miranda is around. She's now tense.

"Heidi," she finally says, her tone completely changing. "I need to tell you something but that is just because I don't want you to be surprised, and—" Before she can even finish that sentence, I'm already lost in her memories, her voice becoming muffled. She saw Jace with Elsie earlier. They were holding hands as they walked into school, talking about the upcoming Sweetheart Dance, and then kissing. My mind gets flooded with memories of my own, knowing that Elsie is the reason why everything changed. I remember seeing her room when I possessed her and finding out about her obsession with Jace. His pictures were all over her walls. Her brother, an angel, caused my death because he wanted his sister to have what she wanted, and now, she does.

I don't realize that I've clenched my fists out of anger until I feel Miranda's cold touch on my hand. I quickly relax my hands and pull away.

"Are you going to be okay?" she asks.

I nod, feeling even more numb than usual. I expected to at least feel jealous, or hurt, but I don't. All I can think about is that I need to find a way to get Jace to see who Elsie really is. Whatever they have going on won't last, and I decide to make the Sweetheart

Dance my deadline. Elsie ruined my life, and I'm determined to do the same to her.

As they sit down on the other side of the cafeteria, I feel like all eyes are on me, and sadly, not because of my stupid shirt.

Jace quickly glances at me, and Elsie puts her arms around him as she glares in my direction. I give him a half smile and look at Miranda.

"I need to get out of here," I tell her.

"No way," she says. "Don't give them the satisfaction of knowing that this bothers you."

But that is the thing. It doesn't bother me. I just want revenge. And yes, protecting Jace is a bonus. But Miranda is right. I don't want to give Elsie the satisfaction. I smile at Miranda, and almost wish I could apologize for wearing this shirt.

CHAPTER 5

HEIDI

he rest of the school day is uneventful. I'm grateful for not having any classes with Jace or Elsie, but seeing them together during lunch was enough to put me in a bad mood. Not needing a conversation starter, I ended up putting my hoodie back on to cover my T-shirt and kept to myself for the rest of the day, staring at the piece of paper with those five names as if that were enough to give me answers. Michaela Petran—vampire; Mathilde Augustine—witch; Roman Bishop—mage. I'm not quite clear on what the other two are, but so far, I see no connection between these names at all. I fold the paper and put it away for now.

When I get home, I go straight to my room with every intention to crawl into bed and watch TV for the rest of the day. Out of habit, I check my computer first and decide to do what I do every day—type the memories I find useful; duplicate it into another blog, knowing that this one will be deleted; and erase the history so it can't be found. But today, when I open the laptop, I find a note on the screen.

PLEASE STOP.

"Zane," I say under my breath.

I quickly put the laptop down and stand up. I open the window and look around. There is no one. There are few things that make me feel any type of good emotion. A few weeks ago, I realized that Zane was one of them—but this time, I feel angry. Angry that I miss him. Angry that I want him around. Angry that he left me again. Angry that he is what he is. I stare at my laptop screen. As my fingers graze the keyboard, I close my eyes and see him here, typing this warning. I sigh and open my blog to see everything gone once again. I find myself writing something else instead, hoping that he will come back and read it. It starts out as a way to manipulate him into showing up and facing me, until anger gets in the way.

I didn't ask for any of this. In two years, I was planning to go away with Jace. I was going to go to dance school. I was going to teach dance classes. Have a family. Maybe follow Jace as he tours around with his music. I had dreams. I had goals. I had a soul mate. I had everything.

Now, everything is gone.

Everything—except for this curse of knowing what I do.

So no, I won't quit. Did you ever stop to wonder if I was meant to still be here? That I was given this ability for a reason? That my purpose is to reveal secrets when they need to be revealed?

I stop typing and look outside before looking back at my computer. My hands start to tremble out of anger. Maybe if I hadn't picked up on his memories on the day I returned, I wouldn't have known just how he feels about me. I wouldn't have started to entertain the idea that maybe I was starting to feel something too—enough that I allowed it to create this void between Jace and me. I clench my fists, debating whether I should just delete it all, but instead, I keep going. I glare at my finger where I should have a cut or at least a scratch.

I don't even understand things that are happening to me.

I think back to the nightmares I have. At least that is what I think they are—I close my eyes at night, and all I remember when I wake up is darkness and fear.

I don't even know what the point of this letter is. Even if you had answers, it's not like you'd share them. I'm not looking for you to fix things. I'm obviously broken beyond repair. And I'm guessing you can't fix what you don't understand. I mean, I know you don't go around bringing people back from the dead.

And you—the only being who knows what happened to me . . . well, the only one I could talk to—you keep leaving, and I keep wondering . . . was bringing me back such a horrible mistake? Is that why you are so afraid to come near me?

I leave it open on that screen, facing the window, and I lay down. I'm determined not to fall asleep. I watch the window, just hoping he will show up.

After a while, my eyes start to feel heavy. I fall asleep, and for the first time since I came back, I dream. I find myself at a beach on a warm sunny day.

"Hello, Heidi." I hear a male voice I don't recognize. I look around, but there is no one.

"Hello?" I say back, but no one answers. I walk toward the ocean, feeling the warm sand against my feet.

The voice goes silent for a moment. Then it starts to cut in and out, before darkness takes over.

When I open my eyes in the morning, my computer is facing me.

Mad at myself for falling asleep, I slowly walk toward my laptop, almost afraid of what I will find.

I put in my password and find that most of what I wrote is gone. There is only one question still on the screen and then the answer.

Was bringing me back such a horrible mistake?

Yes.

I stare at the screen for what feels like an eternity before I slam the laptop shut. I get dressed, and instead of going to school, I run toward Havenwood Heights, the wealthy side of Havenwood Falls, and I find myself hiking into the woods, to the area where I disappeared from. Out of breath, I crouch down against a tree and just sit here, wishing I wasn't brought back.

CHAPTER 6

HEIDI

*P*ain.

A stabbing headache hits me, and I put my hands over my temples, massaging my head. I haven't felt pain since that night. Right now, the pain doesn't last long, but it is excruciating.

"You should be in school." I hear his raspy voice. I close my eyes and stay where I am in an attempt to avoid facing him.

I want to tell him to leave me alone. That he shouldn't have brought me back. That he shouldn't feel like he needs to be around because he did this. But what I read on the computer screen keeps replaying in my head over and over again, and he is right. Me being here is a mistake. I shouldn't be here, and maybe that is why I feel so wrong.

"Heidi?" he says.

I force a smile before I turn around, and when my eyes meet his, I can see fear in his gaze. I try to pick up on any memories he may have. Any signs that he truly believes that I am a mistake, but I don't get anything. At all.

I close the distance between us.

He tenses. The last time we were this close, we kissed. That was right before he took off in a hurry.

I take another step closer. He tenses even more. I grin at the thought that he is so nervous right now; that I have this impact on him. I stop. *This should feel wrong*, I think to myself. *I shouldn't have these feelings toward him. I should be in love with Jace. I should steer clear of Zane, knowing that he can be punished for having feelings for me, and probably even more so for kissing me like he has in the past.* Still, my gaze goes to his lips. Confusion clouds my thoughts. I look down, realizing that my fists are clenched and my nails are digging into my skin. I relax my hands and look up into his eyes.

"Do you think it was a mistake to save me?" I blurt out, curious to see if he will say it to my face.

"I don't regret it," he says in a cold tone.

"That is not what I asked you, Zane. Can you ever just answer a question?"

I cross my arms over my chest and wait.

He stands here and stares at me, watching my every movement. As I look into his eyes, my anger is replaced with fear. *I'm a mistake. Or he wouldn't take this long to answer.*

"Your hair is different," he says.

I roll my eyes at him for his inability to answer my questions.

"Answer me," I demand.

He hesitates. Then sighs.

"I feel that letting you go would've been a bigger mistake," he says as he continues to stare at me.

I chuckle. "And where was your kind when I needed protection?" I snap. "Or was I not important enough to rank a guardian angel of my own?"

He lowers his head. "I'm sorry I failed you," he says.

I rub my hand against my forehead. *Why did I even say that?*

I take a few deep breaths to calm myself down. "You didn't fail me. I wasn't your responsibility."

He ignores my attempt at an apology. "I'm worried about you," he finally says.

I scoff. *Obviously not enough, or he would stick around.*

He tilts his head to the side.

"I don't understand why you are trying to draw attention to yourself," he says. "Is this about Jace?"

I raise an eyebrow at him.

"About you not being together anymore," he continues. "That seems to have an odd effect on you. That is why you kissed me back at the library that night, wasn't it? I thought you were just confused at first, but you were hurt because you had just broken up with him. I understand that now."

"Is that what you convinced yourself of?" I shake my head.

I close my eyes and take a deep breath, then another. And another. It doesn't do a damn thing to calm me down.

I open my eyes and glare at him. I don't tell him it's because somewhere along my screwed up existence, I developed feelings for him. After all, he should already know that, and what difference did that make?

"I'm going home, Zane. This is goodbye," I tell him.

He doesn't answer. He just stares at me. I turn around and walk away.

CHAPTER 7

ZANE

"*D*reaming awake once again, angel?"

I lean my head down and stare at my boots. I spent the rest of the day trying to figure out what I should do, how I can help her move on with her life, and I have nothing.

"What do you want, Gabriella?" I ask without looking back.

"Did you think about whatever it is that you needed to think about?" she asks.

I scoff and look at her. "I tried to talk to her," I say.

"I'm aware," she says. "I was around."

I sigh, and look toward Heidi's window. "She's all over the place, Gabriella. Her body language felt all wrong."

She looks like she's deep in thought.

"What?" I ask.

"Nothing." She pauses. "Well, there was a shift in her when you were around. I think that is why she was confused. I've told you before—something in her changes when you are around. Maybe you should consider getting close to her."

"Only, I can't get close without being able to be with her in a way that I was never meant to be," I blurt out.

I freeze. I should never have said that. I reluctantly look at Gabriella, but she doesn't even look surprised.

"Maybe that's part of your punishment," she says under her breath. "Sorry. I just don't think you have much of an option, Zane. She is getting worse. She is a time bomb. She may wake up one day and decide to say everything she knows. Can you imagine the consequences? She will have half the town wanting her head, and the other half wanting to use her for their own benefit."

I look down, knowing she's right, and this is my fault.

A noise from across the street sends me into full alert mode.

Gabriella follows my gaze to Heidi's front door. Heidi walks out, wearing black pants and a black coat, with a hoodie covering her head.

"I can't say this enough—she does keep things interesting," Gabriella says. "Am I going alone tonight or are you coming with me?"

"You go," I tell her. "I need to get back before they realize I'm missing." I pause. "Please take care of her," I beg, before I'm forced to go back to the last place I want to be, but not before Gabriella stops me.

"Zane?" she says.

"Yes?"

"There are other things I haven't told you."

I freeze and watch her.

"She has made a deal with a witch in town, among other minor things. I had to report some of those. I had no option. There are theories that part of her soul was lost when you brought her back. Our kind is planning to intervene if she doesn't improve."

"Intervene? What does that even mean?" I growl.

She shrugs. "It could be making her and her family move out of Havenwood Falls, and forget everything they've ever known. Although there are theories that it wouldn't work on Heidi, considering she's immune to our abilities. And let's face it—the Court goes to great lengths to make sure things run smoothly. Can you imagine the consequences if they knew one of the residents is immune to the town's memory ward, and that she knows what she does and has no desire to keep their secrets?"

"What is the alternative?" I ask.

Gabriella looks toward Heidi's house. "That would be to correct her fate and undo what you have done."

I shake my head and sit back down, knowing I have no option but to stay.

HEIDI

I rush out of the house as soon as Mom and Dad aren't paying attention. I feel like I'm suffocating. Dinner tonight was awful again. With the memories, the lectures about school attendance, my lack of friends, and my lack of interest in anything I used to love, I just had to leave and clear my head.

When I walk by Burger Bar, I see Jace's car. I can see from a distance that Elsie is with him. I decide to focus my energy on saving Jace from Elsie instead of feeling sorry for myself. At the moment, it no longer feels like revenge. It's for Jace's own sake. I just need to grab proof of how much of a stalker she is.

I make my way to her house and go in through her back door after grabbing the hidden key from under a frog statue—a perk of picking up on memories when I possessed her. I walk into her room, hoping it's still the same. Sure enough, on her walls, there are tons of pictures of Jace. Some of the pictures were of Jace and me; only, she replaced my face with hers. *Creep.* It concerns me even more that she still has all of this up, even after they started dating. I grab my phone and take several pictures of the wall. I contemplate saving them to release anonymously on the night of the Sweetheart Dance.

When I turn around to leave, I find the angel Zane has following me around, standing there, waiting for me.

"What?" I ask.

She moves her hand up and holds it there, palm facing up. "Phone," she says. "Hand it over."

I laugh. "Why should I?"

She looks at the wall, then back at me. "I can't say the girl doesn't have issues," she says.

"Well, obviously," I say.

She sighs, then continues, "She means no harm, Heidi. And as much as you blame her for what happened to you, that wasn't her fault. She had no control over or awareness of her brother's actions."

I swallow the lump in my throat.

"She just loves Jace." She pauses and glances at the wall with disgust. "Maybe a bit too much," she says. "Just let them be. Who knows? Maybe she will help him move on. Unless you're doing this because you want him back," she says as she raises an eyebrow at me.

I shake my head. Jace was my everything. The perfect guy. But that wouldn't be fair to him. Not when . . .

"Has he left?" I ask her, referring to Zane.

She tilts her head to the side. "Does it make a difference?" she asks.

I roll my eyes at her. "I guess he's rubbing off on you," I say when she doesn't answer my question.

"Get home, Heidi. Delete those pictures. Try to . . . I don't know . . . make a friend. Try to move on before you get Zane in even more trouble."

And just like that, she vanishes.

CHAPTER 8

HEIDI

*A*t night, I lie in bed looking sleepily at the pictures I took. Gabriella was right, but I can't make myself delete them. I know it's not because I want Jace back. I just don't want him with Elsie. A small part of me starts to hate this person I've become. I should want Jace to be happy. *What the hell is wrong with me?*

Unable to sleep, I decide that I need to talk to him.

Me: Are you awake?

He replies right away.

Jace: Yeah. I'm still at the music store. Getting ready to leave in about 15 minutes or so

I quickly sit up on my bed, anxious about all the things that could go wrong on his way home.

Me: You have to be careful

Jace: Hmmm. Okay. About what exactly?

Me: Just wait for me at the store. I'll come to you

He doesn't reply. I get up and start to get dressed.

Five minutes is all it takes to hear the engine of his Camaro in front of my house. Angry that he is such a careless fool, I rush downstairs and swing the door open.

"What the hell are you doing?" I ask.

"Well," he says, "I didn't want you to be roaming the streets this late at night, and you seemed off."

I shake my head, grab his wrist, and pull him upstairs and into my room. I close the door behind us, and he looks confused.

"I should probably not be here," he says.

"Because of Elsie?" I ask in a sarcastic tone, and he nods.

"I wanted to be the one who told you," he says. "I just didn't know how to."

"That doesn't matter," I tell him.

"Because you moved on?" he asks, and I scoff.

"What's going on with you, Heidi?"

"I remember what happened to me while I was missing," I say.

"You do?" he asks in shock, and I nod.

"Have you told anyone?" He closes the distance between us.

"No. And I'm not going to."

I start to pace back and forth. He takes a step closer and places his hands on my shoulders.

"What happened?" he asks.

He has to know. He deserves to know at least a variation of it.

"You can't tell anyone. I just want you to know so that you're more careful out there."

He gives me a puzzled look, but nods.

"This town, Jace . . . I was attacked by something supernatural that night. They're everywhere."

I can see the look of concern in his eyes before he pulls me into a hug. He runs his fingers through my hair. "You need to talk to someone, Heidi. I think whatever did happen, it was too much for you to handle, and your mind is just . . . playing tricks on you."

Of course he doesn't believe me. Angry tears fill my eyes. "I can show you. I can prove that I'm telling you the truth."

He pulls away. "Okay," he says. "But not tonight. Tonight, you're staying here, where you're safe, and as long as you are okay with it, I'm staying with you."

I nod, mostly because I'm not sending him off into that in the middle of the night.

He leads me toward the bed and lies down next to me.

I'm at the beach again. There is a guy standing by the ocean, his wings spread wide.

"Zane?" I say, recognizing his build and his clothes.

He doesn't respond. I start to walk toward him when I see a vision of a vampire drinking blood from my wrist. I freeze in place, looking confused. A voice comes through, but I can't make out the words. It's almost as if there is a lot of static muffling the words, then it clears.

"Help us understand. Help us correct your fate."

I make myself take another step forward toward the angel, but he disappears before my eyes.

I wake up feeling hazy. My head is pounding, but the first thing I notice is that Jace is gone. I try to remember what the voice sounded like, but my brain is a complete fog. I shrug it off. *Just a stupid dream.* Knowing that I can't be late to school again, I get up. I see a missed call and a message on my phone.

Jace: Can we talk after school?

I don't reply. I throw my phone on the bed and hop in the shower.

I put on a pair of ripped jeans, my favorite ankle boots, my new shirt, and I'm off to school. Today, I'm wearing my vampire slayer shirt. I figured I'd make this vampire week. Next week may be witches or shape-shifters.

Having a few extra minutes, I decide to stop and grab a hot chocolate on the way. I stand frozen steps away from Coffee Haven when I see Jace and Elsie sitting inside, having breakfast. He's holding his guitar, playing something, and she is smiling. I can't make myself move.

I feel Zane's presence before his hand slips into mine. I can feel tears run down my face, but I don't take my eyes off Jace and Elsie.

"I feel like I'm watching a scene of what my life should've been like right now. I don't think I remember the last time I was that happy."

"That could still be your life, Heidi. I know he was with you last night. He obviously hasn't gotten over you."

I look down at his hand in mine, and I quickly pull away. "I can't."

"Why? What changed, Heidi? Jace was the one thing you missed the most when I was helping you. I thought I'd bring you back and you'd pick up where you left off. That you'd be happy."

I chuckle. "You really don't know what changed, do you?"

He shakes his head.

"You happened, Zane."

He gives me a confused look.

"Last night wasn't what you think. I don't feel that way about Jace anymore. Besides, do you think I just go around kissing people like I kissed you that night?" I ask.

He stands there, frozen.

"But it doesn't matter," I tell him. "You are what you are. So please do what I asked and leave. That would make things easier on both of us."

I turn to the side and give him a kiss on the cheek, then walk away without looking back.

As I walk away from him, whatever I was feeling a moment ago is gone. I start to feel the same as I have every other day— anxious, angry. I pick up the pace, and once inside the school, I take off my sweater.

I don't get far before my vision is blocked as one of the seniors steps in front of me. I know he's a vampire, which makes this so much more interesting. I look up at him.

"Can I help you?" I ask.

"Nice shirt," he says with a smile. "Are you on a vamp kick or something like that?"

"Something like that," I say. "It's more of an all supernaturals kick."

"Interesting," he says as he rubs his chin.

I grin. "How so?"

"What brought that along?" he asks.

I shrug. Miranda swoops in.

"Do you not watch TV?" she asks him. "With all the supernatural shows on right now, how can anyone not be on a supernatural kick?" She giggles and rolls her eyes at him.

He shrugs and leaves.

"So what have you been watching lately?" she asks as we walk down the hall.

"Not much, really," I say, sidetracked by a group of students near us. She notices me looking at them.

"I think they're curious about how you're doing with Jace's situation and all," she says.

"Yeah, maybe."

"How are you?" she asks. "The two of you had been together for so long. This has to be hard."

"It is what it is," I tell her in a harsher tone than I meant to.

She gives me a sympathetic smile. Her memories right now are of me and Jace, together. She really does think I'm acting this way because of him.

It's a boring morning. When lunchtime comes around, I sit as far away from Jace and Elsie as possible and hide behind a book. I'm surprised when Ezra, the new student wearing jeans and a super tight black T-shirt, who also happens to be a vampire, comes in and slides down the seat next to me. The irony, considering the dream I had last night.

I stare into his gray-green eyes.

"Yes?" I ask, looking up from the book.

He grins. "Nice shirt," he says.

I catch glimpses of his memories of drinking blood from an animal in the woods. I try my best to mask my disgust—something that I feel I've been doing a lot of lately.

I roll my eyes at him. "Yeah, it seems to be a great conversation starter."

"Don't you ever wonder what it must feel like?" he whispers. Facing him, I catch him looking at my neck. For a moment, I can't even form an answer. He laughs and looks at my book. "What are you reading?"

"Is everything okay here?" I look over and see Jace standing next to the table. Glancing to where he usually sits with Elsie, I see her watching his every move.

"Yeah," I say. "Elsie seems worried about you, though. Maybe you should get back."

Ezra gives him a half smile, but Jace doesn't move right away. He stares at me as if he's searching for clues that I need to be rescued. I hold his gaze, hoping he will see that I'm okay and leave.

I was so frantic last night, I didn't even notice that I still can't pick up on his memories thanks to the deal I made with Ani, and by the sad look in his eyes, I am glad that is the case. He finally turns around and leaves.

"Ex-boyfriend?" Ezra asks.

"How did you know?"

He shrugs. "Gut feeling. And he isn't over you." He pauses. "And his girl is pissed. He can't seem to take his eyes off you." He chuckles. "This has got to be the most interesting lunch since my first day here last week."

"Look, I'm off the market, so—"

He puts his hands up. "You're direct. I like it!"

I roll my eyes at him.

"Relax. You're not my type."

"Really?"

He nods. I pick up on a memory of him kissing another guy. "Let's just say that your ex would be more my type than you are." He winks at me.

"Oh. Okay."

"Just looking to make some friends. As interesting as your shirt collection is, you don't seem to have many either."

I shrug.

"So, what are you into, besides vampires?" He laughs. If he only knew what I know . . .

"Not much lately. I used to be into ballet, but I haven't really gotten back into it since I— Well, it's been a while." I realize that talking to someone who doesn't know my past may not be that bad.

"Do you miss it?" he asks.

"Haven't really stopped to give it any thought. What about you?" I ask.

"I have a common interest in vampires." He chuckles.

"Of course you do," I say in a sarcastic tone.

He leans in my ear and whispers, "You know, don't you?"

For a split second, I freeze in place.

"Know what?" I ask.

He grins and winks at me. "Hey. What are you doing after school?" he asks.

"Going home and sulking."

He laughs. "I'm coming over. I need someone to show me what there is to do around here."

"What? Aurelia isn't showing you around?" I ask, knowing that he's staying with the Petran family, and that Aurelia, who is in a few of my classes, is by far one of the most bitter and bitchy girls in the school.

His expression goes serious for a minute. "You're kidding, right?" he asks, and I shrug.

"Yeah, she's been such a delight to be around," he says in a sarcastic tone.

I open my mouth to say something when he stops me. "I won't take no for an answer, and trust me—I can be very compelling." He winks again.

"I need to take care of some things, now that I think about it." He actually looks disappointed. *Ugh.* "I guess meet me in town square at five?"

CHAPTER 9

HEIDI

I fully intended to stand him up, but as five gets closer, I decide to take Gabriella's advice to make new friends. I remind myself that it will be nice to have someone around who doesn't know much about me.

I get to town square right at five and find him waiting for me. He is sitting on a bench, looking at his phone. He looks up as I get closer and grins. "I have to admit, I totally thought you were going to ditch me."

"I considered it," I say in a serious tone.

He chuckles. "I believe it. Why did you decide to come?" he asks as he nods toward the bench. I sit next to him.

"I don't know," I lie. A part of me has been craving a friend to talk to. Jace had always been that person. I'd been with him since middle school, and we always had our own thing going on. We had friends, but at the end of the day, we were each other's best friends.

He gives me a half smile.

"I told you I had a compelling personality," he says with a smirk.

Ezra catches me staring toward the music store where Jace works. We can see him inside, by the door.

"You know, I heard he was asking questions about me after lunch. He obviously still cares."

I give him a sad smile.

He bumps my shoulder with his. "Want me to help you get him back?"

I wish people would stop assuming that is the case. I shake my head. "No. He needs to move on. I just wish it was with someone other than his current girlfriend."

"Do you want to tell me why the two of you broke up?" he asks.

"We both needed space. Things weren't the same after I got back. We just grew apart."

"Got back from where?" he asks.

"Long story," I say in a cold tone.

"Is there someone else?" he asks, and I hesitate. "Someone from our school?" he asks with a smile.

"I wish. It's not that simple."

"Is anything ever simple?" he asks, laughing.

"Used to be," I say as I look down.

"So, what is the deal with the hair change?"

I look at him and raise an eyebrow. He just started school last week and we didn't even talk until today. I'm surprised he noticed.

"Just needed a change," I say. I start to feel like I'm under interrogation. "I know nothing about you. Start talking," I say, even though I know enough about him, but only through his memories.

Ezra tells me he was sent here to live with family after he got into some trouble at home in Romania. He won't talk about the reason, but from his memories, I know it was about his boyfriend and his dad not being so accepting of his lifestyle.

"We have an audience," he says. I look at him, and he nods toward the music store. Jace is standing at the door, looking over in our direction. I get a text.

Jace: Can I talk to you, please? Only 5 minutes.

I look up from my phone and see Jace watching me.

Me: Maybe another time.

He reads it, puts his phone away, and walks back into the store, looking upset.

"Let's get out of here," I tell Ezra.

"Where to?" he asks.

I shrug. "Somewhere away from people. I don't really feel like being around anyone right now."

He tilts his head to the side. "Thank you?" he says. "I guess I should feel honored."

I chuckle. "I hope your shoes are comfortable," I say, and he gives me a puzzled look.

I lead Ezra toward the Mills mansion.

"Good Lord, girl. You could have warned me we were going on a hike, ya know?"

I shrug. "You look like you're in good shape. Figured you could keep up."

We keep going until we reach the wooded area I'm always so drawn to.

Grateful that the ground is clear of snow, I sit down with my back against a tree, and he sits across from me.

"Interesting choice of place," he says as he looks around.

I get hit with a horrible headache again. I rub my temples. I see flashes of images of the beach and someone drinking from my wrist. They stop at the moment the pain goes away.

"You okay?" he asks.

I nod. "Yeah. Just a headache."

～

ZANE

Heidi walks toward a boy on a bench.

"Who is that?" I ask Gabriella as we watch Heidi from a distance.

She looks up from her freshly manicured nails. "Ezra

Dimitrius. He's Michaela Petran's cousin. He recently moved here from Romania."

"Okay? What's Heidi doing with him?" I ask.

She shrugs. "I did tell her she should make new friends. Maybe she finally listened to something." She pauses. "This is good, Zane."

"Not an ideal choice when his cousin is a member of the Court," I growl.

Heidi and Ezra stand up from the benches, and we follow from a distance.

"What is she doing?" I say out loud as they walk into the woods.

Gabriella looks as intrigued as I do. "Let's get closer," she says.

"We can't. She will see us—hear us."

"I took care of that," she says. I give her a puzzled look, but before I can ask anything, she's already next to them. I kneel down next to Heidi. I close my eyes for a split second realizing how much I missed this—the ability to be this close, to protect her.

"Can I ask you a question?" Heidi says, looking at Ezra.

"Sure. But only if I can ask you something first," he says as he plays with a piece of grass.

She shrugs. "Go for it."

"How do you know about—hmm—you know . . ." He lets his shoulders rise and fall. His lips part, and he runs his tongue over his teeth.

I freeze. "She just met him, and he already knows that she's aware of it all!" I growl.

But Heidi hesitates in answering.

"How did he find out?" I whisper.

"I won't tell anyone," he says.

She shrugs. "Let's say I'm psychic or something like that. I can pick up on things people have done."

I shake my head, fighting the urge to make myself visible right now and get her out of here.

"And that doesn't freak you out?" he asks.

She shakes her head.

"That is kind of neat," he says.

She scoffs. "It's hell, really."

"Does anyone know?" he asks.

"No," she lies.

"How does that work anyway?" he asks. "Do you pick and choose whenever you want it to work?"

"That is way more than one question," she says in a cold tone.

He nods. "You're right. Your turn."

She grabs a piece of paper from her pocket and leans forward to show it to him.

"What do these names have in common?" she asks. At first, even I don't make the connection. Ezra's eyes widen.

He stares at it for a while.

"I'm not answering that," he finally says in a tense tone. She gives him this wicked grin that is not quite like her.

Members of the Court of the Sun and the Moon, I think to myself. *The governing body of the supernaturals and the rest of the town.*

I look over at Heidi. I know every feature—every look—every single detail about her. So I instantly notice when her eyes darken. She looks distant. Her tone changes slightly—she almost sounds more . . . well, like she's reading off a script someone gave her.

"Have you ever bitten someone?"

"No," he says.

Her eyes go back to normal. She looks confused for a split second before they darken again. "Aren't you curious about what that would be like?" she asks.

He gives her a nervous smile. "That is more than one question."

She nods and looks away, but his gaze is on her. Studying her every movement.

"Sure, I'm curious, but I would never."

"How come?" she asks.

"Things would not end well. I could lose control and kill the person, for one thing."

"But you don't know that," she says with a grin. He stops to think about it but doesn't say a word. She goes on. "Okay, humor me for a minute. You feed from animals and bottles, right?"

He nods, looking confused.

"Okay. And when you are drinking you can stop when you want, right?"

"Yes," he says, with a puzzled expression.

"It can't be that different," she says.

"What is she doing?" I say out loud. Gabriella stands next to me. "Look at her eyes, Gabriella."

She does. "I told you something is off about her. It's not just about Jace, or about things changing."

"What are you getting at, Heidi?" Ezra asks.

"I want you to drink from me," she says. "I want to know what it would feel like."

I'm in complete shock at first, and that is what gives Gabriella time to stop me from making myself seen and throwing Heidi over my shoulders to get her out of here.

"Relax," says Gabriella. "He would never. There are consequences for both here. Just let this play out."

I glare at Gabriella.

"She will be okay," she says. "You're right here, after all. We both are."

Ezra laughs. "Not a chance."

"I wouldn't tell anyone."

He looks uncomfortable. "Why would you even want that?" he asks.

"I told you. Curiosity."

He shakes his head. "I can't, Heidi. There is no way."

She smiles at him, but even her smile is off. She lets it go, but I know the idea is planted in his head now.

CHAPTER 10

HEIDI

*M*y heart races as curiosity consumes me. Curiosity that goes far beyond what Ezra probably thinks. I wonder if he actually said yes, if I would heal as quickly as I did when I cut my finger. *Why am I not afraid?* Images from that dream invade my memory, almost as if it is a way to ensure me that this is what I should be doing.

The walk back is awkward. We both walk in silence, and I'm pretty sure I won't hear from him ever again. By the time I get home, it's already dark. Mom and Dad are watching TV, and I tell them I already ate. I go straight to my computer and open my blog. I grab the piece of paper from my pocket and open it, placing the paper in front of my screen. Through Ezra's memories, I have just what I needed. These are five of the people responsible for keeping the supernatural around here safe. If I expose them, it could be my chance to keep the humans safe. I open a new page and start typing.

A little over a year ago, my whole life changed when I realized that everything about the place where I grew up was a lie. My name is Heidi Bennett, and I grew up in Havenwood Falls. If you're reading this from somewhere outside of this town, it is pretty likely that you've never heard of Havenwood Falls. Even if you have been here before.

Don't worry. I will explain the reason shortly. And if you live here, and you are like me—someone who grew up in a lie—you won't believe me at first. But that's okay. If you just take the time to search for the truth, you'll see that I'm right.

As my eyes start to feel heavy, I decide to take a quick break. I close my eyes and start thinking about Ezra.

I fall asleep thinking about our conversation. What if he did lose control? Would that correct my fate? Why does this feel so right when it should be everything but?

Darkness.

I find myself at the beach again. The same angel stands by the water.

"Zane?" I ask.

The voice comes—still muffled. "He's coming for you. This is your purpose. Do not back out."

I jump awake, almost dropping the laptop. I look around my room. At first, I'm in a daze, wondering who will show up. My heart leaps at the thought that maybe it is Zane. I shake my head, knowing that I can't keep wishing for that. This is why I sent him away. We can't be near each other. As much as I wish otherwise, he is what he is, and the thought of him being punished even more because of me—

I hear something hit my window.

"What the hell?" I say. I go to the window and see Ezra on the street. I rush down the stairs and open the door.

He just stands there, looking nervous.

"Come in," I say. "Quietly. You don't want to wake up my parents."

He awkwardly comes in, and we go up to my room.

He keeps his distance, and he looks tense. I can't even pick up on any of his memories—it's as if he is too nervous to even think.

"You're staring at my neck," I tell him.

"Were you serious about your offer?" he asks, and I shrug.

"Sure."

"Why?" he asks. "The real reason."

"Let's say I have limits of my own to test."

He pulls something out of his pocket.

"What's that?" I ask.

"A taser," he says nervously. "I want you to use it on me if I don't stop—or if you feel weak, or weird about it all."

I take it from his hand. "Sure," I say, knowing that I don't even know how to use the thing.

"Are you ready?" he asks, and I nod.

He takes a step closer to me. I watch his every move, analyzing his body language, the way he looks at me. I'm almost disappointed that I'm not confronted with some sort of cold and predatory look. He looks terrified, really.

He stops. "I can't do this."

I roll my eyes at him, grab a pair of scissors from my desk, and put it against my wrist. "Do you need motivation?" I ask.

"Please, stop," he begs. "I don't know what I was thinking."

"Why are you so hesitant? Isn't that what your kind does? Drain humans of their blood?"

He shakes his head. "I don't know what's wrong with you right now, but you don't even know what you're talking about."

"Explain," I command, still holding the scissors to my wrist.

His hands are trembling. "Can you put the scissors away?" he asks nervously.

"Eventually," I say in a cold tone.

"I'm what you call a moroi. I don't feed from people. I'm sure you can do your psychic thing and confirm it. If I took one sip, I could lose control and turn into something I dread. I could lose my soul, and if caught, which in Havenwood Falls I'm certain I would be, I would be executed."

"How do you know?" I ask. "How do you know you would turn into something that you're not?" I ask.

He looks down. "Because that's what happened to my mom."

"But you came here tonight," I tell him. His eyes are now on the scissors as they make a dent in my skin.

44

ZANE

I do a quick check-in on the poor soul I should be watching over. As always, he's sitting in his room, playing video games.

"Nothing is happening here," I tell myself before I rush back to Havenwood Falls. Gabriella is sitting on the roof, reading a magazine. I glance over at Heidi's, and her lights are on.

"What's going on?" I ask, as I see two shadows through the curtains.

She looks up from the magazine.

"Uh-oh. I thought she was sleeping. I got distracted."

I don't wait on her to say anything else. I make myself unseen and rush into Heidi's room. I find Ezra on one side of the room, looking terrified. Heidi is on the other side, holding a pair of scissors in her hand. Her eyes are even darker than earlier. She pierces her skin, and at the sight of blood, my gaze goes to Ezra. His body language shifts. He no longer looks terrified. He launches toward her. Making myself seen, I cut him off, grabbing his neck with my hand.

"Zane!" she says. I look at her while not letting go of him.

Her eyes are no longer dark. She looks like she's on the verge of tears. "I'm sorry. I'm so sorry. This wasn't his fault. I promise. Let him go. Please," she begs.

Ezra looks scared again.

I let go of his neck.

"Sit," I order him, and he does.

I rush toward Heidi and grab her hand. I watch her wrist heal right before me, then I look into her eyes.

"What's wrong with me?" she cries.

I pull her into a hug.

"Can someone tell me what's going on here?" Ezra asks, his voice shaking.

I run my hands through her hair as she sobs against my chest.

I tell him a very loose variation of the truth. "Heidi went missing some time ago. She doesn't remember what happened to her, but she's not been quite herself lately."

Ezra nods.

I expect the boy to be eager to leave—to just run and do who knows what with that information—but I know I can trust him the moment he looks at me with a concerned expression and asks, "Is there something I can do to help?"

"Other than not sinking your fangs into the girl?" Gabriella asks as she shows up.

Ezra looks apologetic.

"Just don't talk about it with anyone," says Gabriella. Heidi's hold around me tightens.

Gabriella looks at me. She crosses her arms over her chest. She looks down at Heidi, and her gaze goes to my arms around her.

"You have a choice to make, angel," she says in a warning tone.

"I can't," I tell her.

"I have to report this, or it's my head."

Heidi sobs even more.

"I can't protect her if I'm not what I am," I growl.

She sighs. "Outside. Now."

I slowly pull away from Heidi.

I glare at Ezra, not too sure how I feel leaving her alone with him.

"I'm fine," he says. "I will stay with her until you get back."

I nod, then look at Heidi, but she avoids my gaze.

Gabriella and I go back to where we usually sit. She stands with her arms crossed, tapping her heels on the roof.

"You're forgetting that you have me to help you—the two of you. But you have to choose, Zane. You're at fault for all of this. We can't explain what happened, but there's one thing I'm certain of. She's more grounded when you're around." She pauses. "There are other ways to protect her. You being what you are is doing more damage than good. To everyone."

I nod, understanding that I put her in a bad position.

She sighs. "In a way, I'm a little jealous."

"Jealous?" I scoff. "I spend my existence in a constant battle between protecting her and trying to keep my distance from her so as not to break the rules that were imposed on me. Jealous of what, exactly?"

"I just wish I could remember what it feels like to be in love," she says. "But Zane—" She gives me a warning look. "You should've walked away from what you are when you first fell for her. Make your choice. I will help protect her—even if it comes to protecting her from our own kind. Although I don't think that will be necessary once you're around her in a way that both of you need."

I look toward Heidi's house.

"I choose her," I say, feeling the relief that these words bring me. "In a way, I always have."

CHAPTER 11

ZANE

I expected to feel different. I expected to feel shame for turning my back on everything I know. I expected to feel regret. But I don't feel any of that. I feel relief that I finally acted on what I knew a long time ago.

I know I won't be able to do so many things that I have always had the ability to do before, and my biggest concern is that those will become weaknesses when it comes to protecting Heidi.

The weirdest part of it all is probably seeing Gabriella's happiness over it. Her acceptance of my decision was a nice surprise, and her promise to help protect Heidi was a relief.

Gabriella takes me to the hallway that leads to Heidi's room. My invisibility is gone and so is my ability to get places like I used to.

The house is quiet. I know Heidi's parents are sleeping, but I can hear her and Ezra in her room.

"I'm sorry," she tells him.

"It's okay. I lost count of how many times you apologized, but I already told you countless times that I forgive you. Just don't do it again, okay?"

I walk in then. For a split second, she looks confused, then it hits her.

"Why?" she asks.

I ignore her question. "I need to ask you something," I tell her. I look over at Ezra.

"Hmm. I guess I should go?" he says.

Heidi gives him a sad smile.

"I promise. It's fine," he says, knowing how bad she feels about what she did. "I'll see you later, okay?"

She nods, and he leaves.

"What's going to happen to you?" she asks as soon as the door closes.

I close the distance between us. "It's you that I'm worried about."

She chuckles. "I see that your inability to answer questions is still there."

My gaze goes to her lips. I wonder if it would feel any different to kiss her now—without all the guilt. But this is not something I'm going to find out tonight. When I do kiss her again, I want everything to be perfect.

"I know you weren't in control earlier," I tell her. "I could see it in your eyes." I pause. "That list of names you've been carrying around. How did you get it?" I ask.

"From Ani Rukska," she says.

Angry with myself for not realizing this before, I take a few steps away from Heidi. My tone grows colder. Angrier. "Gabriella mentioned that you made some kind of deal with a witch. Is that the one?" I ask, knowing that a spell is one possible cause for whatever is going on with Heidi.

She nods.

"What was the deal?" I ask.

She looks away. "To block people's memories from me, and—"

"And?" I ask.

She looks up at me, and she hesitates.

"To make me forget you." She looks away, avoiding my gaze.

It takes me a minute to process this. She continues, "In

49

exchange, I was supposed to check into certain people's memories for her."

"Okay, did she call off the deal? Obviously none of it worked."

Heidi shakes her head. "She tricked me. She blocked Jace's memories from me. That part worked. Forgetting you was impossible."

I grin at the way she says that last part.

"Don't let that go to your head," she says.

Focus, I tell myself. "What happened next?" I ask.

"I told her I wasn't going to do what she asked. She tricked me and the deal was off. I used the list of names she gave me as leverage."

My hands clench into fists.

"Where does she live?" I ask.

She pauses. "Do you think she has something to do with what's happening?"

"I don't know," I tell her. "But it's the only lead I have right now. Why on earth would you make a deal and then confront a witch, Heidi?"

"It didn't seem fair that she did that. If you're right, what can we do about it?" she asks.

"I'll fix the problem," I tell her, but truthfully, I have no idea what to do here. Every option leads to more people finding out about Heidi's abilities.

Heidi hesitantly gives me directions to where the witch lives, and I have to make her promise me to keep her distance, and not do anything stupid while I go search for answers. I decide not to tell Gabriella, knowing that there are certain things she would have to report—and this witch abusing her powers would be one of those things, which leads right back to more people, more angels, finding out about her.

It's two in the morning when Heidi walks me out.

"This is weird," she says. "You not just disappearing right in front of me."

"I know," I tell her.

"Are you coming back?" she asks.

I nod.

"Why did you do it, Zane? Why did you choose me? I'm not the same person I used to be."

I smile at her. "Yes, you are. Or you wouldn't have felt bad about Ezra. You wouldn't be asking me this question now, or be worried about what happens next. That night, you just got lost in more ways than you know. I'm going to help you get back to where you were before."

She closes her eyes for a split second and sighs. When she opens her eyes again, I'm closer. Reason tells me to turn around and leave, but I feel a pull toward her that can't be denied. As much as I want everything to be perfect—as much as I know I need to get it together and focus—deep down, I know I won't be able to do that until I kiss her. So I give in. I lean in and kiss her, and for the first time, without the world's weight on my shoulders.

I make my way to the witch's house without seeing a soul around, which I'm thankful for, considering that everyone can see me now. My plan is to wait until morning and catch her on the way out. I'll pretend that Heidi did the same to me as she did to her—getting a favor without fulfilling her side of the deal—and then, hopefully, she will share more information on what she has done out of revenge.

There are not many houses around hers, but I'm surprised to see that the lights are still on and music is blasting.

The music stops.

"Bring me another," I hear a male's voice I recognize all too well, as he yells his request. I clench my fists.

"No," I growl.

I walk slowly toward the house, wanting to confirm before I go get Gabriella to report his location. I move quietly to the window on the side of the house, and there he is. Bryson—the dominion angel behind Heidi's disappearance that night. He holds a beer in his hand, and his other hand is on the witch's lower back as she laughs hysterically. He drinks and jokes. He then takes a long swig of his drink and hands her the bottle.

"Get me another, will you?" he asks, and when she moves, unblocking my view, there is Gabriella, sitting on the recliner, sipping on a red drink while she comfortably looks through a fashion magazine.

CHAPTER 12

ZANE

I have to fight the urge to go in there, because right at this moment, there is nothing I can do. Not against all three of them, and not with my lack of powers.

I walk back to Heidi's house knowing that there is only one thing I can do. I will have to call on one of the elders, tell them everything, and hope they can help fix this and let Heidi be. That is the only way I know how to protect her. That is, if they even answer my call.

On the walk back to her, I keep wondering why Gabriella would do this. I decide not to confront her. Not yet, anyway.

I just want to spend one normal day with Heidi before this is all over.

The sun rises, and I wait until her parents leave for work before I go in. I sit on her bed and wake her up. Her eyes are dark once again.

She sits up, closes her eyes, leans her head down, and takes deep breaths.

"What's wrong?" I ask.

"Bad dream," she says.

"Do you want to talk about it?"

"No," she says, looking at me. Her eyes are back to normal. "I don't remember most of it. It was dark. I remember seeing trees. There was a voice trying to say something, but his speech was slurred."

Of course. This must be how the witch and Bryson are getting to her, I think to myself.

"Did you find the answers you were looking for?" she asks.

I don't want to lie to her, so I ignore her question. "Why don't you get dressed? I want to take you somewhere today."

She gives me a confused look.

"It's a surprise. Come on." I smile. "I'll wait outside. Wear something comfortable."

"Hmm . . . okay," she says, looking even more confused.

Fifteen minutes later, she walks outside wearing yoga pants, tennis shoes, and a coat.

"Is this good?" she asks.

I nod. "Perfect."

"Where are we going?" she asks.

"First, breakfast."

As we walk down the street, I slip my hand into hers. She smiles up at me.

I lead her to Coffee Haven, knowing how much she likes going there. I realize that wasn't the best choice when she's ordering and Jace and Elsie come in, hand in hand.

"They are *together?*" I ask in a whisper.

"Ugh. Yes," says Heidi. "Unfortunately."

The barista gives us the total, and I feel bad when Heidi pulls out her wallet to pay for it. Not being used to being seen, I didn't even think about this.

Jace interrupts. "I'm paying for hers," he tells the barista.

Heidi and I look back at him.

"You don't have to," says Heidi.

"I want to," he says.

He looks over at me then.

"I remember you," he says, referring to the night at the library when he caught us kissing. "Just know that if you hurt her, you have me to deal with," he warns.

I nod, feeling awkward. Not just because he basically threatened me, but because for so long, he was my assignment.

"Can we just go?" says Elsie. "I'm not feeling well."

Elsie doesn't look sick. She looks mad. He pays for Heidi's order, then smiles at her, and they leave.

"How can I even compete with that," I say. Not meaning to say it out loud.

Heidi smiles. "It isn't a competition, Zane."

We eat, then we walk toward the dance studio. Heidi's eyes widen as soon as she realizes where we are going.

"I told you I was going to help you get back to where you were. You used to love this."

The disappointed look on her face throws me off. I stop walking.

"What is it?" I ask.

She sighs. "What happens when . . . if . . . I do get back to where I was? Will you leave again?"

"Never," I promise.

She goes from disappointed to shocked.

"What?" I ask.

She laughs. "I just can't believe you actually answered a question."

CHAPTER 13

ZANE

"*I* don't even have dance shoes," she says as we walk into the studio.

I look at her and smirk. "Just give me a few minutes."

I ask to talk to the owner, and I go into her office while Heidi waits. The owner tells me how much she missed having Heidi around and thanks me for bringing her in. She says classes are not until later in the day, so we're welcome to use the main room. When I ask if she happens to have extra ballet shoes around, she walks toward a cabinet in the corner of the room.

"Do you know her size?" she asks.

"Seven," I tell her, and she grabs a brand new pair.

"Come on," she says. "I want to welcome her back."

She smiles from ear to ear when she sees Heidi.

Heidi looks distant and maybe a little nervous. She pulls Heidi into a hug before giving her the ballet shoes.

"Please don't disappear on me again," she says. "We really missed having you here."

"You did?" Heidi asks.

"Of course!" she says. "I hope today means that you will be returning to classes soon?"

"I . . . hmm . . ." Heidi stutters. She looks at me, and I smile at her. "Yes, of course," she says.

"Well, I told your friend here that you can use the main room. Just yell if you need anything, okay?"

Heidi nods, holding tightly to the dance shoes.

I follow her as she walks to the middle of the main room. She looks at her reflection in the mirror before looking down at the shoes she is holding.

"Do you want me to leave you alone?" I ask, but she shakes her head.

She takes off her coat, throwing it to the side. She then sits on the floor, takes her shoes off, and puts on the ballet shoes. She stretches her legs out.

"How does it feel?" I ask her.

She smiles. "Like I never stopped. Thank you, Zane."

I give her a short nod and extend my hand to her. She slips her hand into mine, and the moment I pull her up, her arms instantly go around me. I hug her back, and we stay like this for a while.

"Are you ready to do this?" I ask.

She slowly pulls away and nods. She turns the music on, and I sit on the floor, against one of the mirrors. She twirls around as I watch her. At least an hour goes by without us even realizing. I could watch her all day. When she stops dancing, she looks back at the door. I follow her gaze and see the studio's owner watching her.

"Perfection," she says. "No rush. You can have the room for another thirty minutes, but make sure you stop by my office before you leave so we can get you registered for classes." She pauses. "I'm not taking no for answer."

Heidi looks so much lighter, happier.

She goes back to the middle of the room and lies down. I lie down next to her and slip my hand into hers.

"Why did you do it, Zane? Why did you give up everything?" she asks, looking over at me.

"I didn't give up everything, Heidi. I have you."

She blushes. "Wow. That was pretty smooth for an angel . . . or, well . . . that was smooth."

I chuckle. "You forget I read romance novels. I learned a thing or two."

She laughs.

I watch her. I missed that smile. I missed that laughter that comes from pure happiness.

"For so long I hated what I was—or at least the rules surrounding it all," I tell her. "From the day I first saw you, that part of me was already gone in a way. I hated feeling guilty for loving you."

I see that her eyes have widened.

I sit up. "I guess I just said one of those things that scare humans away, didn't I?" I pause. "I didn't mean to scare you, and I definitely don't expect you to feel the same about me."

She is sitting up now, too. She leans in and kisses me.

We spend the afternoon together. After sunset, I walk her home, and we stop by her front door, where we kiss again.

At the sound of someone clearing his throat, we pull away, and find Ezra staring at us.

"Am I interrupting?" he asks with a grin.

"Yes," Heidi and I both say at the same time.

"I don't understand why you are not running as far away as possible from me," says Heidi.

"Are you kidding me?" asks Ezra. "Aurelia was driving me insane. I needed normal people to hang out with."

"Normal?" Heidi asks while laughing.

Ezra shrugs. "You're not as bad as you think."

"Well, I guess, come on in," Heidi says, and we follow her to her room.

I sit on her bed, and Ezra sits by her desk.

"Hey, do you mind if I use your computer? Aurelia gets in a mood whenever I try to borrow hers."

"Is she ever not in a mood?" Heidi asks. "Go ahead," she says.

Heidi sits next to me. Ezra opens her laptop, then he goes quiet. When he finally turns around, he looks horrified.

"You haven't shared this anywhere, have you?" he asks. "You can't do that!"

Heidi tenses. I stand up and walk toward the laptop.

"I haven't," says Heidi. "Not yet."

Ezra moves from his seat and sits next to her, and I quickly click the delete button after scanning through it. When I turn around, she is staring down at the floor.

"I don't know just how much you are aware of, Heidi," says Ezra, "but the Court is there to *protect* the town. That includes humans."

She scoffs.

"My cousin, Michaela, told me about your disappearance when I asked her about you. Everyone was looking for you, Heidi —vampires, werewolves, shifters—everyone!" he says.

"They were?" Heidi asks with tears in her eyes.

"Whatever really happened, you can't blame everyone in town because of one bad apple, Heidi."

"But I don't remember ever picking up on memories of anyone searching, other than Jace and my parents. And the sheriff, but he is kind of obligated to do it."

Ezra puts his hand over hers. "I can promise you they were looking. My cousin would never lie about something like that. Not that cousin, anyway." He laughs. "Just let it all stay in the past. You got this cool ability. You got this hot guy," he says, making me uncomfortable. "Just forget the past."

She nods once.

Then she stands up, and I notice the shift.

"Heidi?"

"I have somewhere to be," she says. "I'll see you later, okay?"

"Where do you have to be? I'll go with you."

She rolls her eyes at me. "Come on, Zane. Don't be the clingy boyfriend. I just have somewhere to be. I will see you later," and she takes off. I'm left with no choice but to follow her.

"Stay here," I warn Ezra.

When she starts to go into the woods, I rush and get in front of her. "Where are you going, Heidi?"

She ignores me and keeps walking. I stop her. "I will throw you over my shoulders and carry you if I need to," I warn her.

She chuckles. I inch toward her with every intention to do as I said, but it's too late. Bryson, Ani, and Gabriella are standing behind her.

CHAPTER 14

ZANE

I quickly move and stand in front of Heidi, blocking her from their view. A part of me thinks that Heidi won't stay behind me, so I'm surprised when I feel her hold my hand. Her hand is ice cold, and I can feel her tremble.

My gaze narrows on Gabriella.

"Why?" I ask.

Her lips curl into a smile. "I'm merely doing what needs to be done, Zane."

"And that would be?" I growl.

"To correct her fate. She shouldn't be here."

"Actually, this is exactly where she should be. If anyone made her deviate from her fate, that was him," I say as I glare at Bryson.

Heidi's grip on my hand tightens.

"It's not just that. This connection that you have is an abomination. You should not have fallen for a human. And her—knowing what you are and still pursuing you—well, that is just as bad, if not worse."

"It's not up to you to judge," I tell her.

She looks over at the witch. "Now," she says.

The witch says a few words I can't understand, and next thing I know, my whole body starts to feel heavy. My hand involuntarily lets go of Heidi's, and I stand, frozen in place, held up by the witch's magic. Then my vision goes dark. I open my mouth to tell Heidi to at least try to run, but the words don't come out. I'm completely helpless.

"Bryson, get the girl," Gabriella says in a calm tone. I hear Heidi scream my name. I can feel her touch, but I can't do anything. I just keep thinking, *Run, please. Leave me and run!*

Everything goes quiet.

"I have her," Bryson whispers in my ear right before I hear Heidi cry in pain.

Stop! I growl, even though I know they can't hear me.

I hear Bryson's voice again. "How does it feel to know that I'm going to get rid of her again, and there is nothing you can do about it? You failed her once, and you're going to fail her again. Only this time, you are standing within inches of her."

I'm not losing her again. I can't lose her again. Please. I beg anyone who is listening. *Save her. I will go back. I will take whatever punishments you deem fit. Just save her.*

Silence. There is not one sound.

Then I hear Ezra yelling my name. "Zane! Zane!" He pauses. "Crap," he says.

Everything goes silent again, but not for long. The sound of Ezra talking to someone else warns me that it's all over. Everyone who shouldn't know about Heidi will know about her now.

"Michaela," he says in a desperate tone. "I need your help . . . Heidi is in trouble. Three people took her. Her boyfriend is here, but he's out of it. It's like he's frozen or something . . . No, not Jace. Zane . . . Come on, I'm new here, and *I* know that. Keep up, cousin . . . Where am I? Well, that is another problem. I have no clue. I followed them into the woods. I couldn't tell you how to get to where I am . . . uh huh . . . Yeah, I don't have a point of reference. All I see are trees and snow. Hey! I have an idea! I could use their prints on the snow to track them!" I can hear Michaela yell at him to stay where he is. "Yeah, I have the find my phone thingy on, but I'm in the middle of nowhere . . . Okay."

I can feel Ezra poking my arm, then pull on my jacket.

"Zane, if you can hear me, I'm following the footprints to try to find Heidi. Michaela is coming. I put my phone in your pocket so she can find you. Hopefully."

Part of me wants to yell at him to stay put. The other part is grateful he is going after Heidi. Either way, I can't do a thing about it.

Some time goes by—maybe minutes, but it feels like forever. As I begin to feel my body again, I drop to the ground on my knees. When I regain my vision, I see one of the elders, Zelia, in front of me. I frantically look around to find two other angels behind me. A young woman with brown hair comes running up behind them, her gray-green eyes searching all around me.

"Where's Ezra?" she asks.

"He went after Heidi." I slowly stand up.

"What happened?" Zelia asks.

I keep looking toward the footprints.

"We don't have time for this right now. Help me find Heidi first. Please," I beg. I look at Zelia. "Can you track Gabriella?"

The elder nods.

"Heidi was taken by Gabriella, Bryson, and a witch," I tell them.

I can see by their expressions that they all have questions, but they don't waste time asking. Michaela just watches our interaction curiously. Seconds later, the elder takes us to the back of the witch's house.

Looking through the window, we see Ezra and Heidi both tied up, with their backs to one another. Gabriella, Ani, and Bryson stand in front of them. Heidi shakes her head at something they tell her, and that's when Bryson grabs Ezra by his arm, pulling him up.

The angels, confused, look at one another. "We are not

supposed to intervene," says one, and my mind goes right back to what Gabriella said about correcting Heidi's fate.

"We're not waiting," says Michaela.

I couldn't agree more.

"Take the front door," I tell her. "I'll take the back."

When I burst in through the door, I come face to face with the witch trying to run.

"You're not going anywhere," I warn her, closing the door behind me. I grab her by her arm and go toward the living room. When I step into the room, I see all three angels. Zelia stands in front of Gabriella and Bryson, who are kneeled down in front of her. One angel is tending to Heidi in one corner of the room as the other angel and Michaela tend to Ezra.

I let go of the witch's arm and rush toward Heidi when I see how hurt she is. I reach for her arm, where there is a large cut, which leads me to understand why they are keeping Ezra on the other side of the room. Michaela watches Heidi curiously, and her eyes widen as she sees Heidi heal right before her eyes.

I help Heidi up and put my arms around her.

"I'm sorry," she says.

"This isn't your fault," I assure her.

Zelia gives Heidi a sympathetic look before her gaze goes back to the other angels. "Take Bryson and Gabriella, please. I will deal with them later. Make sure they're supervised." She looks from them to Bryson and Gabriella. "At all times."

"Okay, who's going to tell me what's going on here?" Michaela asks, looking from Ezra to Heidi. "Ezra?" She lifts a brow in a warning look.

"He doesn't know," Heidi says. "I will tell you everything."

I nod over toward the back door—the witch shouldn't know more than she already does.

"Not here," I say. "Let's go outside."

Michaela glares at Ani, opening her mouth to speak.

"She will not be going anywhere," Zelia says.

Michaela looks from her to Ezra. "Stay here, please. Keep an eye on Ani."

Ezra nods.

When we step outside, Michaela crosses her arms over her chest. "What happened?" she asks, looking at Heidi.

Heidi gives me an apologetic look. This will change everything. I hold on to her hand.

"Go ahead," I tell her. There is no getting out of this now.

Heidi sighs. "That night I went missing, I was hurt by an angel. I died a few months later," she says.

Michaela keeps calm as she listens to everything. Heidi tells her about how she was stuck here as a ghost, and that after she moved on, I brought her back to life. Michaela looks at me then with such intensity, I almost want to run. Still, she doesn't say anything. She crosses her arms over her chest but keeps listening as Heidi tells her about her power to see people's memories. Michaela's eyes widen then, and she starts to put things together.

"And Ani knew about that?" she asks.

Heidi nods. "She gave me a list of names. She said she wanted me to find out what I could about them."

Heidi pulls the paper from her pocket and gives it to Michaela. Michaela stares at it.

"And you know what these names have in common?" she asks, and Heidi nods.

"Have you told Ani anything that you know?" Michaela asks.

Heidi shakes her head. "Nope. And that is how I ended up here tonight."

Michaela nods and looks down at the paper as if she is deep in thought—trying to figure out what to do.

"Why didn't you?" Michaela asks.

Heidi looks down. "I wish I could say it was because I wanted to do the right thing, but . . . it was out of revenge."

Michaela looks surprised.

"I asked her to erase my memory of Zane, and—" Heidi stops. "It didn't work," she says.

Michaela nods. "Do you know if she actually tried to erase your memory?"

Heidi gives her a puzzled look, and I take a step forward, standing in front of Heidi.

"You will not erase Heidi's memories," I warn Michaela. "Even if you try, it won't work. There is a lot that Heidi is immune to." I pause. "She will leave your secrets alone. She won't get involved with anything supernatural. She just wants to be left alone. We both do."

Michaela pulls her phone out of her pocket, and I tense. She dials a number, "Hi, Ric, It's Michaela. I need you to send one of your guys to pick up Ani Rukska from her house, and we need to have an emergency meeting."

She hangs up and looks at Heidi. "I want you to stay with Ezra until I can talk to the others. Can he stay at your house? Just give me a few hours, and we will call you."

Heidi nods.

Sheriff Ric Kasun is the one who comes to pick up the witch himself. Michaela goes with him, leaving Ezra with a list of instructions, which includes not letting Heidi out of his sight.

When they leave, Zelia walks toward us.

I let go of Heidi's hand and take a few steps away.

"I'm sorry," I say, looking down.

"Never apologize for how you feel." Zelia tilts her head to the side as she looks at me. She smiles. "Not when the feelings are so pure."

"But I shouldn't—"

She cuts me off. "Yet you do, son. I trust there is a reason for that. I'm not here to judge you, or to punish you."

She looks at Heidi then and reaches for her hand.

"May I?"

Heidi nods.

Zelia closes her eyes. When she opens her eyes again, she looks saddened.

"I'm so sorry that all of this happened to you. That night should never have happened." She pauses. "This gift that you see as a curse—I can't take it away from you, but I can help you control it."

"Thank you," Heidi says.

Zelia sighs. "I just wish that something could be done to make up for our errors."

Heidi looks down. Her tone lowers. "There is something," she says in almost a whisper.

Zelia tilts her head to the side. "Go on."

"Please let Zane stay," Heidi begs.

CHAPTER 15

ZANE

*T*hings start to change almost immediately. After arriving at Heidi's house, Heidi and I tell Ezra everything. Once he knows the whole story, Ezra calls his cousin and begs her to let him be at that emergency meeting and to vouch for Heidi not being a risk to anyone. Michaela makes him sit out for the first part of it, but once she allows him in, he tells them how Heidi just wanted a second chance at life, especially since she met me. It's enough to get Michaela on our side. Maybe some of the others too. And it doesn't hurt that the members of the Court have all known Heidi since she was little. Their only request is that Heidi attends Sun and Moon Academy to learn about the supernatural world and her abilities.

In Havenwood Falls, things couldn't be better. Now we wait to hear from the angels.

Several days after the Court meeting, Heidi shows up at her dad's store a few minutes before my shift is over. Yet another change since that night. Heidi introduced me to her parents as a friend who's new in town and in need of help. They know I'm not just a friend. I can sense that miles away, even without any abilities of my own. I think they're just glad she sounds more like herself and has someone in her life. Her parents gave me a job at their store and a room to stay in at their house.

"What are we doing tonight?" she asks, as I finish stocking one of the shelves.

"I thought I could take you out," I say. "Your dad gave me an advance on my first check."

"I love that you want to do that," she says, "but I don't feel like being around people." She lowers her tone. "I wish Zelia would just ask a witch to block everyone's memories from me, like Ani did with Jace."

"Well," I say, "that is unnatural, and unnatural usually means bad consequences."

She rolls her eyes at me. "Yeah, yeah . . ."

"Just keep practicing the exercises she gave you to control it. Between her help and the Academy, you'll get this. It just takes time." I finish up and look toward the back. "Mr. Bennett?"

"Yes?" her dad says.

"I'm done here. Is there anything else you need done?"

"That'd be it. Thank you, Zane. Go. Have fun."

We leave the store and head to Coffee Haven, where Ezra is meeting us.

On the way, Heidi stops me.

"Do you really think they will call on you or come for you, like Zelia said? She seems nice, but I don't get why they would do that. Can they make you leave?"

I move a lock of her hair behind her ear. "If that happens, just know that I will make my way back to you."

I can tell that doesn't make her feel any better, but she drops the subject. I just hope I can keep her mind off it.

Ezra is already waiting on us when we walk into Coffee Haven, and he has Heidi's favorites already ordered, waiting on her.

Heidi pulls her sweater over her head, and Ezra spits out his drink from laughing so hard. When she faces me, I just shake my head.

"Really?" says Ezra. "Did it have to be that one?" he asks, referring to the *Vampires suck* shirt. She smiles, and suddenly, it's all worth it.

Her smile turns into a frown when a group of students I don't recognize walk in, talking about the Sweetheart Dance. I catch Heidi staring at them, looking distant.

I bump into her shoulder. "Do you want to go?" I ask.

Ezra kicks me under the table and shakes his head, and Heidi gives me a confused look.

"To the dance," I continue.

"Nah," she says. Then she excuses herself and goes toward the restrooms.

I look at Ezra, who is giving me an evil look. He looks down when I meet his gaze, but I get the feeling there is something he wants to say.

"Did I say something wrong?" I ask.

He nods slowly. "Just a little. Don't feel bad, though. Most guys would make the same mistake."

"What did I do?" I ask as I raise an eyebrow at him.

He puts the napkin down. "It was the way you asked her. Don't ask her to go just for the sake of asking. I know she was with Jace for quite some time, and from what I heard people say, he used to make a big deal out of everything. I mean—you were there for most of it, right? You gotta know you have big shoes to fill. Put some thought into it. Show her that you want to take her to the dance. That you can't imagine spending that night any other way than with her by your side."

Okay, maybe the kid has point.

"Do you have any ideas?" I ask.

He leans in and tells me what he has in mind.

I laugh. "There is absolutely no way I'm doing that. Why purple anyway?"

He shrugs. "It has something to do with a town legend I heard about—a witch who had two great loves. It actually reminds me of Heidi—with you and Jace. No offense."

I roll my eyes at him. "I never heard of it," I say as I look back, wondering why Heidi is taking so long.

"Well, I like my idea. You should go for it. I'll even take care of everything. You just have to stand there and look hot."

I shake my head, looking embarrassed. "Nope. And you're insane. This is the most ridiculous idea I've ever heard."

Ezra smirks and shrugs. "Worst case scenario, it would put a smile on that girl's face. I don't see how that can be a bad idea."

"What did I miss?" Heidi asks as she sits down.

"Nothing," we both say.

We finish our drinks, then Heidi has to get to dance class. Another thing her parents were so happy about, and so is she.

I offer to walk her to the studio, but she refuses, saying she could use some alone time to clear her head.

Ezra and I stay at Coffee Haven, and it's not until she leaves that I spot Jace sitting at a corner table, watching us. Once she's gone, he stands up and walks toward us.

"Hey, man, can I talk to you?" he asks.

"Sure," I agree, even though I'm certain he will punch me at any minute. "So . . . ?" I say.

Jace puts his hands in his pockets and shifts his weight from one foot to the other, looking uncomfortable. Finally, he says, "I just want to ask you to take care of her. No hard feelings. I want Heidi to be happy, and she's more like herself when she's around you."

I nod. I can see in his eyes that he means the Heidi that he fell in love with—that he's still in love with, even though he's with Elsie. I have a whole new level of respect for him for saying that.

When he walks away, I turn to Ezra.

"Swoon!" says Ezra. "Too bad he's straight."

I roll my eyes at him. "Fine. We'll do that stupid idea of yours."

He smiles from ear to ear. "I'll take care of everything. Just meet me outside the dance studio ten minutes before she gets out."

I pace in front of the studio. Five minutes before she gets out, Ezra shows up. I don't even know how he was able to find these, and in a way, I wish he hadn't. I heard some of the guys in town talking about their "man cards," and I'm pretty sure this leads to me losing mine.

And so here I stand, holding purple pig balloons and a poster that says, "When pigs fly, will you go to the Sweetheart Dance with me?"

Ezra grabs his phone. "Smile" he says. I don't, but he takes the picture anyway.

"I'm going to kill you," I say.

He laughs. "This is a little comical—a guy with your build, combat boots . . . holding that."

"Ha," I say in a sarcastic tone. I put the sign down. "Here," I try to hand him the balloons. "There is no way I'm doing this. It's ridiculous!"

"Too late. She's coming. Hold that sign up, boy." He laughs.

I think it takes her a minute to get it.

"RELEASE THE BALLOONS!" says Ezra.

I do, and she bursts out laughing, before she rushes in my direction and wraps her arms around me. She then looks at Ezra.

"Your idea?" she asks, and he admits to it proudly. "What's the deal with the pigs being purple?" she asks.

Ezra looks at me.

"Oh no," I say. "You tell her that one."

He laughs. "Fine. I heard this town legend about a witch and something to do with purple pigs. From what I heard, she had two loves, and it kinda made me think of you."

She raises an eyebrow at him. "First of all," she says in a playful tone, "the word *witch* traumatizes me a bit. And based on the legend, her two loves were her china and her pigs, and she went crazy at some point." She pauses. "What part exactly makes you think of me?"

"Oops." He laughs. "That's not what I heard."

She rolls her eyes at him, and I stand here watching how happy she looks. Finally, she meets my gaze.

"So, is that a yes?" I ask.

She nods with a huge grin on her face.

CHAPTER 16

HEIDI

*T*he night before the Sweetheart Dance, I head to my room right after dinner to do homework. I find a note on my bed.

Meet me at the library at 8?

I feel my stomach churn. Zane was supposed to stay late and help with inventory tonight, so this can't be good. I rush to the library. I get in and go to the second floor, where we used to spend so much time. I find Zane standing in the middle of a room full of books, wearing a suit. There is soft music playing. He turns on a lamp and stars dance around the room.

I look around, amazed. He walks toward me and extends a hand. I slip my hand into his, but as much as I want to be in the moment, I know something is off.

"What's this about?" I ask.

He looks intensely at me without saying a word. His hand goes to the small of my back, and he slowly pulls me closer, leans in, and kisses me.

When he pulls away, I look at him, waiting for him to say

something . . . anything. When he doesn't, I know what this means.

"You're leaving again," I say. And I hate that it doesn't make me love him any less.

He nods. "I have to. They want to talk. But I promise you that I will be back."

"Let me go with you," I say.

He looks down, and I swallow the lump in my throat.

"You miss it, don't you? Having a purpose? I don't blame you. For a while, I missed that too."

"Heidi, you have a purpose. Your life shouldn't have been interrupted. You should be here now. You are here. Take advantage of that. And believe me. I'm not letting you go. I'll be back."

Out of desperation, I resort to a childish attempt to keep him here. "How do you know I'm not going to the dance tomorrow and will do something crazy? Maybe spread the truth about Elsie like I had planned before, and maybe others too—"

He cuts me off. "Because that wasn't all you, Heidi. That was Bryson and Ani and Gabriella messing with your head. Do you even still have those pictures you took at Elsie's house?"

I shake my head. "No. I deleted them all."

"I know you. You are good. You understand that none of that was Elsie's fault. Yes, she went a little psycho with the pictures on the wall, and I know you're worried about Jace, but—" He pauses. "Go to the dance tomorrow with Ezra, and have fun. For me. I'll be back as soon as I can."

"Why don't I believe you?" I ask.

"Because I don't have the best track record. But it's different now. I already walked away from it all, and I don't feel an ounce of regret. This is where I should be. With you."

ZANE

Before leaving, I make Ezra promise me to take her to the dance if I'm not back on time. I hate leaving her, even if temporarily, but I feel that I owe Zelia, and I want to make sure Heidi will be protected.

Zelia comes to get me. I fully expect to be taken in for a lecture and requests for my return, but instead, I find myself in a room full of angels. Bryson and Gabriella are kneeled down in the middle of the room.

"Come," Zelia tells me, and I follow her to the center. We stand in front of Bryson and Gabriella.

"Thank you all for being here today," Zelia says. "Yesterday, we went over everything that happened. Bryson and Gabriella have confessed to allying with a witch to control Heidi Bennett and to influence her through her dreams. Are there any objections to Zane weighing in on their punishment?"

My eyes widen. I don't know how to do this. I've never had such responsibilities. Yet no one objects.

"Zane?" she says. "What do you suggest?"

I stop to think about it. Still shocked that I'm face to face with the ones who put Heidi through so much, I'm inclined to show them some mercy.

I sigh. "I believe they shouldn't be allowed around humans again."

Zelia nods.

I think of Heidi's concern for Jace. "And I believe that my last assignment—Jace Edwards—would be better protected if away from Elsie Brooks," I say. At that, Bryson growls.

Zelia smiles. "I believe that is fair. Take him away," she tells one of the other angels.

"And Gabriella?" she asks.

I grin and tilt my head to the side. "I believe that Gabriella has become too infatuated with certain things from the human world. She should suffer enough if she's kept away from things like fashion, gossip magazines . . ."

Gabriella glares at me. I smile. Some of the angels chuckle.

"Very well," says Zelia. "We'll add that to her final sentencing, which we will discuss later. Now, about Heidi."

"What about Heidi?" I ask in an alarmed tone.

Zelia gives me a genuine smile. "I believe the girl means no harm to others. She was depressed and dealing with the shock of the tragedies she was put through. Bryson, Gabriella, and Ani's alliance only made things much worse. And due to our mistakes, she lost faith. We believe that you, Zane, healing and bringing her back has made her immortal, which will not be a problem—at least for a couple of years. Does anyone disagree that Heidi is not a threat and should be left in peace?"

Relief washes over me as no one speaks.

Then I ask the question about the one word that stuck in my mind. "Immortal? How?"

Zelia keeps her focus on me. "A lot about what happened to Heidi leaves us with questions. She died many months before you brought her back, Zane. You shouldn't have been able to revive her, unless you had special abilities of your own that affected her in unprecedented ways." She pauses. "Now let's talk about you, Zane," she says.

One of the angels speaks. "Will he finally be charged for bringing her back?"

The room falls silent again, and Zelia continues as if no one has spoken. "Zane has served his time. That is the end of that." She then looks at me. "Zane, it has come to my attention that you may have been coerced by Gabriella into making a choice. Was that what you truly wanted?"

HEIDI

Ezra makes sure I go to the dance. He insists and says that Zane made him promise a million times over.

I wear a black dress that Mom bought for me. Ezra picks me

up, and Mom and Dad take a billion pictures. When they ask where Zane is, I say he had to take care of something personal.

"He will be back," I say, as if trying to convince myself that he is actually coming.

As soon as we walk into the open warehouse-style building, the Annex, I spot Jace by one of the food tables, alone. I wave a quick hello, and he walks up to me with a smile on his face.

"Uh-oh," says Ezra. "I'm not sure what to do here. Should I pretend to be your temporary boyfriend so he will back off?"

I laugh at him. "Relax."

Jace gets closer.

"Where is Elsie?" I ask.

He chuckles. "It seems that I have this horrible bad timing when it comes to dances and telling girls that I'm getting ready to move."

I raise an eyebrow at him.

"Dad just got a call about an hour ago. He's getting transferred to New York in a few months, and it makes sense that I live there. As a songwriter, there are just more opportunities."

"Wow. That's amazing, Jace."

"Where is Zane?" he asks.

"He's away for a while," I say.

"Oh."

"He'll be back," I say awkwardly. "Congrats on the move, though. I'm happy for you, Jace. I know you will do amazing things." I'm also happy he will be away from Elsie, but I don't tell him that.

"Well, do you want to dance?" he asks. I look from him to Ezra.

"Go for it," says Ezra. "Just don't forget who your real date is."

I roll my eyes at Ezra before Jace and I walk away.

We dance to a slow song.

"Hey, what is it that you wanted to talk to me about?" I ask.

"Nothing," he says. "It doesn't matter anymore."

I hear him chuckle.

"What?" I ask as I stop dancing and look at him.

He nods his head toward the entrance. "I guess he couldn't stay away from you too long."

He gives me a sad smile. I stand here, staring at Zane at the door as he stares back at me. I look from Zane to Jace, not knowing what to say.

"Go," he says. "You deserve to be happy, Heidi. Always did. It just sucks I'm not part of the picture."

Tears well up in my eyes.

He gives me a half smile. "Go!" he says.

I pull him into a quick hug before I walk toward Zane. I stop about two feet away from him. He closes the distance between us.

I shake my head. "You have this horrible habit of leaving, and every time you come back, I feel like I've fallen for you even more," I say.

He grins. "Should I leave again?" he asks.

I laugh. He takes a step closer, wraps his arms around me, and whispers in my ear, "I'm here to stay. I choose you, Heidi. I always have."

We hope you enjoyed this story in the Havenwood Falls High series of novellas featuring a variety of supernatural creatures. The series is a collaborative effort by multiple authors.

Other books you might enjoy in the Young Adult Havenwood Falls High series:

Awaken the Soul by Michele G. Miller
Forever Emeline by Katie M. John
Saving Infiniti by Rose Garcia
Willful by Liz Ferry

Stay up to date at www.HavenwoodFalls.com

DANIELE LANZAROTTA

ABOUT THE AUTHOR

Daniele Lanzarotta is the author of young adult and new adult paranormal, fantasy, and contemporary novels, including the Academy of the Fallen Series, the Sudden Hope novels, and A Mermaid's Curse Trilogy.

Daniele is also a filmmaker and CEO & Founder of Elysian Nightfall Studios—a brand development, audio & video production, and film company. She has recently worked on Virginia-based short films as the Second Assistant Director and Still Photographer. Daniele is currently working on the development stage for the adaptation of her novel, *Sudden Hope*, which she also plans to film in Virginia. She is also working on other film and writing projects.

She enjoys watching hockey, playing Rock Band and Guitar Hero, and spending time with her husband, two daughters, and the family dog.

For more about Daniele and her novels, please visit www.danilanzarotta.com

ACKNOWLEDGMENTS

It takes a village.

Thank you, Kristie, for allowing me the opportunity to be a part of this world. I fell in love with Zane and Heidi when I wrote *Avenoir*, and I'm thankful for the opportunity to share more of their lives.

Thank you to all the Havenwood Falls authors for the amazing communication and collaboration.

I can't wait to see what the future holds for Havenwood Falls!

AN EXCERPT

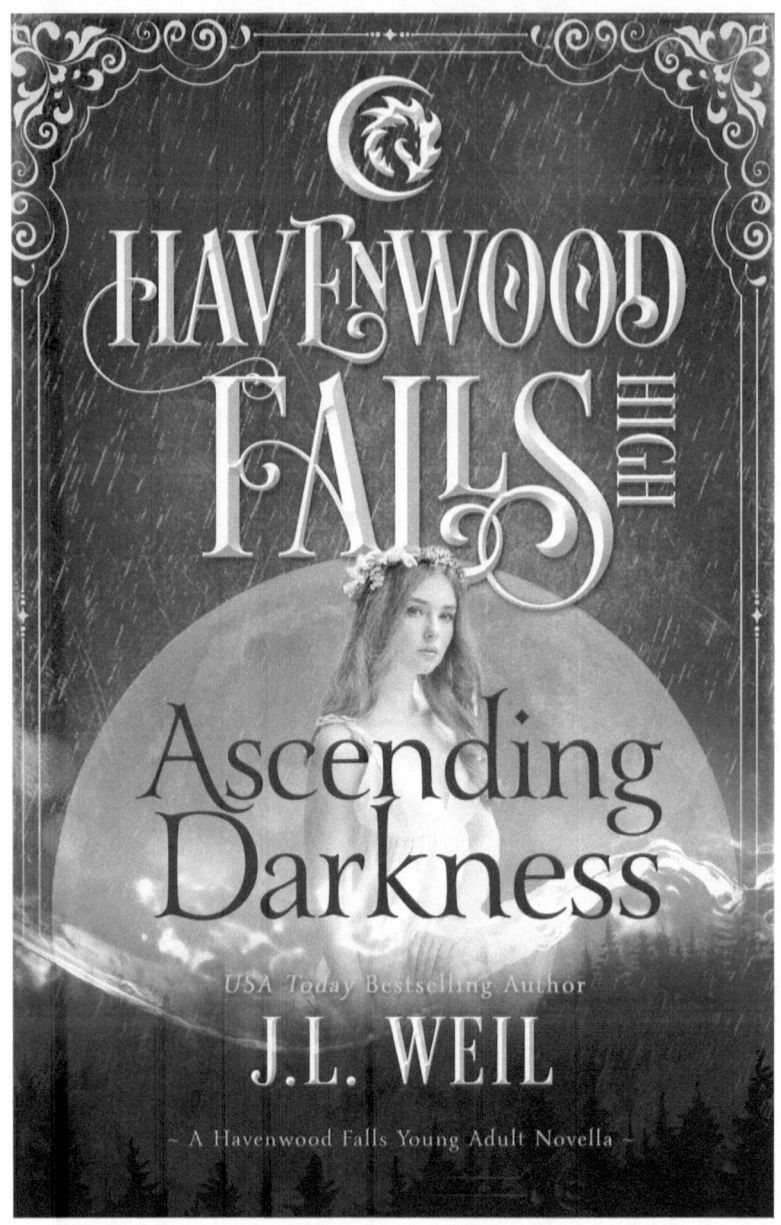

Ascending Darkness (A Havenwood Falls High Novella) by
J.L. Weil

**From *USA Today* bestselling author J.L. Weil comes the sequel
to *Falling Deep*, where the truth can be a dangerous game.**

Mallory Dorian only wanted a normal, boring life. To
graduate high school, go off to college—basically, do everything
the opposite of her mom. But life has a way of interfering with her
carefully laid out plans.

Insert Torent Stark, the drool-worthy demon who makes her
want to throw away all her dreams. But before Mallory can open
her heart, a dark shadow of death looms inside.

Mallory must face the past before she can think about the
future, and her family's history has a few dark spots. It is up to her
to break the blood curse looming over her family or risk all that
she has grown to love.

ASCENDING DARKNESS

BY J.L. WEIL

The window in my bedroom was closed and yet, for an instant, I smelled the sea, heard the call of the water, felt its coolness wash over my face. Here and then gone. The longing to be in the water swelled in my heart, like an endless love.

Not that I knew a lot about love.

Why Torent Stark's face instantly flashed in my head at the mention of love was something I'd rather not dwell on. In fact, I'd rather not think of him at all. Too bad my mind didn't feel the same way.

Torent was a boy.

Okay, he wasn't just any boy. First, he was a half-demon. That right there was a giant red flag waving in my face and should have been enough to tell me he was bad news. Then there was the crazy ex-girlfriend drama. Torent's ex-girlfriend had made me her archenemy. Sometimes too much baggage was not worth the risk, but my heart didn't seem to care about his past relationships or the dark streak inside him he worked so hard to hide and control. I gave him mad props. He had so much more control over his abilities than I did.

My magnetic energy was still unstable, causing inconvenient outbursts, like the time a box of staples almost embedded itself into one of my instructors at Sun and Moon Academy during one of my night classes.

What I was going to do about Torent was another one of those mysteries of life, and damn if my life hadn't become a long Nancy Drew novel. So much secrecy shrouded my past, and I was only recently unearthing the answers, but I had more questions.

Before moving to Havenwood Falls, my life was normal. I'd lived in Wisconsin, gone to an average high school, watched my mother end yet another marriage. And in a way, things had returned to that habitual norm. Mom got a job, which Gigi was thrilled about. I had settled in at school and was coming to terms with being a water nymph.

Okay, so not your typical normal, but my life was average by Havenwood Falls standards.

However, some things never change.

Take Brooklyn Kendall, for instance. She still hated my guts. Turns out she didn't need a magical object to feel such strong enmity for me.

Torent was still trying to get me to go out with him. He was persistent—I'd give him that. And cute. And charming. And . . .

A bird squawked outside my window, interrupting my internal list of all of Torent's redeeming qualities. At this time of the year, the local birds had already migrated south, but a few stragglers had taken up residence in the tree outside my window. They had spent the last week waking me up before my alarm, and that put them on my shit list. I was not a morning person, not before at least two cups of coffee. I hadn't thought much about it, but this morning, something about the sound gave me the heebie-jeebies.

My eyes narrowed, and I went to the window to push aside the curtain and peer out into the yard. The sun was just peeking over the mountains and, it being late November, the air would be brisk. A light sheet of snow carpeted the grass.

Perched on an icy branch, the black bird gave another warning screech. His midnight feathers were in stark contrast against the barren tree. Beady eyes of charcoal watched cautiously through the glass. Strange. His feathers ruffled as he stretched out his wings, and I smiled, tapping lightly on the window.

"Where are all your little friends?" I asked, not really thinking about the fact I was talking to a bird.

He cocked his head to the left and right, eyeing me. Then he kicked off the little branch and flew straight into the window. *Thwack.* I jumped back, unable to believe what had happened.

The bird had just committed suicide.

A blotch of blood smeared down the glass, and my stomach turned. I backed away, feeling uneasy about what I'd seen. It wasn't every day I witnessed a bird snapping its own neck.

So much for that *normal* life.

My cell phone buzzed on the bed, and I turned my back to the massacre streaming down my window to pick up my phone.

"Crap," I grumbled, staring at the time on my phone. My third alarm had gone off, and if I didn't move my ass, I would be late for school.

I tossed on a pair of jeans, a white tank top, and a flannel, only to stop in front of the mirror. *Dear God, is that me?*

My hair looked like one of those black birds had made a nest in it, blond curls messily framing my face. The mascara I was too lazy to remove last night was smeared over my eyes, giving me a Goth look. I was going to have to roll with it. On my way out the door, I snatched a tube of lip gloss and applied it hastily to my lips, then sprayed two squirts of perfume over my clothes, unsure if they were clean or not. I grabbed a brush, my car keys, and my book bag before dashing down the stairs into the kitchen.

Gigi was sipping a mug of hot coffee.

"Morning." She grinned cheerily.

I grumbled an inaudible response and plucked her cup of coffee from her hands, downing half of it. "Thanks. I needed that."

"I guess so," she replied, taking back the nearly empty cup. Her blue eyes were shining. For a woman in her sixties, Gigi was sharp as a whip.

Mom came around the corner and stopped halfway to the coffeepot, eyeing me. "What happened to your hair?"

She was dressed in black slacks and a white button-down shirt, one button too many undone at the top. No one was more shocked Mom had gotten a job as a file clerk at Bishop Enterprises than Gigi.

The two of them constantly harped at one another. It was as routine as taking the garbage to the curb on Wednesdays.

"Don't ask," I mumbled, moving through the kitchen. I threw a hand in the air, waving bye, and stepped out the front door.

Icy breezes wrapped around me, and a blast of wind blew through my flannel. I cursed myself for not grabbing a to-go mug of coffee. It would be a long-ass day. Not to mention what this wind was doing to my already disastrous hair.

Jogging down the stone path to my old and semi-reliable car, I twisted my head toward the tree outside my bedroom window, my thoughts returning to the bird. I didn't have to time check on his little corpse, and yet I found myself moving off the path and onto the lawn. The frozen grass crunched under my weight. I grew closer, and eventually my Converses skidded as my steps faltered.

What the—

There wasn't just one poor dead bird under the aspen tree. There were at least half a dozen strewn over the cold ground, their small necks angled oddly off to the side. My heart knocked in my chest.

My hand flew to my mouth, and I took a step backward. A trickle of unease ribboned down my spine as I tried but failed to make sense of the scene in front of me. What had happened here? I wanted to believe it was a natural event, not something supernatural, but I couldn't shake the sneaky suspicion it wasn't Mother Nature at play.

God, it would be just like Brooklyn Kendall to arrange a bird graveyard to freak me out. Things between my fellow water nymph and me were anything but smooth sailing. She still wanted to make my life miserable and blamed me for pretty much everything wrong in her seemingly perfect life. Misery loves company, as the saying went.

I suppressed a shiver and got into my car, backing out of the driveway with enough speed to kick up gravel.

I whipped my car into the parking lot of Havenwood Falls High. The three-story red brick building was bustling with students rushing to get to class. Throwing my car into park, I sat staring at the arched front doors and considered skipping the entire day. The whole dead-bird thing had gotten to me, more than I realized.

But ditching classes would earn me a Saturday detention and would tarnish my pristine college resume. I had a plan. That plan didn't involve me being stuck in Havenwood Falls for the rest of my life.

A world existed behind these mountains and waterfalls, and I was going to see it all. I *was* going to get that college scholarship. No deranged pranks or cute boys were going to stop me from pursuing my dreams.

I dashed through the front doors as the bell for first period rang. Son of a bitch. I was late. Again. My feet flew over the brown marble floor toward my first class. No time to stop at my locker.

"I hope this isn't going to become a weekly occurrence, Ms. Dorian," Mr. Zander, my AP English Lit teacher, scolded while I was sneaking not so stealthily into class.

I slumped into my seat, a tight smile pasted on my lips. "I wouldn't dream of it."

He went back to waving the black marker in the air, telling the class to open their textbooks to page seventy-three.

What a way to start the day.

I managed to get through my morning classes. Silver and blue snowflake decorations lined the cream hallways for the upcoming holidays. There always seemed to be some school event going on. HFH's mascot was a dragon. How fitting. The fierce-looking dragon was plastered everywhere—floors, walls, banners, flyers—you name it and he was there.

I slid my butt into the seat across from Beck, who was picking at something under his nails. Someone had given his hair color a boost last night. The blue was extra bright today.

"You know I'd dye your hair for you," I said, grabbing one of his hands and surveying the damage to his fingers. The skin was tinged blue, along with the tips of his nails.

He pulled his hand back to his side of the cafeteria table. "It looks so damn easy in the commercials."

I rolled my eyes. "You're supposed to wear gloves."

His nose wrinkled in disdain. "They make my hands sweat."

My brows rose in question. What was the big deal with a little hand sweat? It beat having blue fingers for a week.

"Wolf thing," he stated. "I was thinking of painting my nails black anyway."

Beck Winslow was the first real friend I'd made in Havenwood Falls. He was also a wolf shifter. Not a big deal in a town full of supernaturals.

I pushed aside some of my wayward second-day hair. "You're not going to believe the morning I've had."

"Hello, blue fingers," he replied, waving his hand in the air. "There is definitely something funky in the atmosphere. I'd say we're in for a snowstorm. I can smell it." His eyes shifted to the large square window that overlooked the parking lot.

That wasn't quite what I had in mind, and despite the sun beaming this morning, an incoming storm would explain the hint of water I sensed in the air. My eyes followed his, seeing the beginnings of gray clouds rolling in. "Is weather predicting a wolf thing?"

He grinned, and it lit up his face. "Intense senses."

My fingers drummed on the tabletop beside my untouched salad. What had possessed me to get rabbit food when what I really wanted was an entire pizza from Napoli's?

"I might need to borrow your intense senses," I said, half joking.

Beck plucked a cherry tomato from the top of my lunch and popped it into his mouth as he leaned over the table. "What's up?"

I nibbled on my lower lip instead of my salad. "This morning, a bird flew into my bedroom window, but that wasn't the strangest part. When I left for school, there were half a dozen dead birds scattered outside my bedroom. Tell me that is normal?"

"*That* is a bad omen, chica."

"Peachy," I said dryly. "Just what I need. So you're saying I should be worried?"

He shrugged. "It's hard to say. This time of year the animals get a little restless. It could be nothing. Oooor," he dragged out, "you might be cursed. Piss someone off lately?"

I sighed and leaned my head into my hands. "That narrows it down."

His eyes spanned the lunchroom, landing on a trio of girls giggling annoyingly. "I can think of one particular popular girl who would love to throw a flock of dead birds at your house."

In sauntered the bitch of the hour.

Brooklyn Kendall.

Would she really do that? Yes, although it didn't explain the bird flying into my window. But the other birds dead on the ground? I wasn't sure. The whole thing smacked of some devious plot Brooklyn would concoct.

The devil herself was giving me a mad case of the stink eye as she crossed the cafeteria with Leena and Cora in tow.

"Is this feud between us ever going to end?" I muttered.

Beck's sparkling gray eyes trailed the nymph squad. "I hope not."

I playfully smacked him on the arm. "Dude, that's not funny."

He rubbed at the spot on his bicep, grinning. "I can't help it. Things have been so much more . . . colorful since you moved in."

My head tilted to the side while I regarded him. "What's the name of your therapist again? I think it might be time to switch your meds."

He laughed, throwing back his blue head and gaining the attention of a few tables surrounding us. "See, this is what I'm talking about. This school needed you, Mal."

I wasn't so sure about that. Brooklyn blamed me for ruining her life. Her ex-boyfriend was derailing me from my life plan. Mom put on a brave face, but I could tell something had her worried. And I had unruly magnetic powers. None of these were things I construed as good.

~

Storms never really bothered me. Maybe it was my connection to water that offered calm during the howling of the winds, the crash of thunder, and the spears of lightning slashing across the black sky. Beck had been right. Havenwood Falls was in for a helluva storm, and for the end of November, ice was definitely in the forecast. For now, the sky was putting on quite the show.

I raced across the parking lot to my car, my bag jostling behind me. The last place I wanted to be caught was on the road when the mixture of rain and ice decided to fall. My steps faltered at the sight of Torent leaning against my Chevy Malibu, and dammit if the car never looked so good. He had a way of making everything around him hotter.

Sighing, I walked around him and opened the backseat door, tossing in my bag.

"What are you doing?" I asked, spinning to face him.

He boxed me in with his body, pressing his palms on either side of the car. My breath hitched at his sudden nearness. *Don't think about how close he is or how wonderfully intoxicating he smells.*

I sank into the cold metal of my car, but it didn't help. My senses went into overdrive. I hadn't been exactly avoiding him, but more or less evading temptation. Damn him and his sexy demon dimples.

"I missed you," he replied in a deep and rich voice that melted over me.

Be strong. You can resist that smirk.

"Torent," I groaned, making the mistake of putting my hands on his chest. They were supposed to push him away, yet ignoring the command my brain sent to my hands, they rested over his beating heart. When was I going to accept that I didn't want to avoid Torent or only be his friend?

He grinned, tugging on the end of a frazzled curl. "I love it when you say my name."

I leveled him with a stare that did absolutely nothing to wipe the wickedness from his violet eyes. Tiny flecks of gold were sprinkled in those irises—his demon. I'd only seen Torent lose control once, and although it had been scary, I hadn't been frightened of the darkness that lived within him.

"You're never going to give up the chase, are you?"

"Not when I want something," he crooned.

It was a thrill to hear he wanted me. I couldn't deny the rush his silky words gave me, but I wasn't impulsive or reckless. I'd thought of little else the last few weeks than what my life would be like if I dated a demon.

"What happens when you get bored?" I challenged, although this wasn't the first time we'd had this conversation. It seemed we were doomed to spin circles around each other.

His nose brushed over the tip of mine, bringing our lips too close for comfort. I only had to tilt my head an inch up and I'd be doing the very thing I longed for—kissing the shit out of Torent Stark. One of his hands lifted off the car and trailed down my arm to lace our fingers together. I shocked myself by letting him. In fact, I wasn't sure I could let go.

"Never going to happen, crash car. There's something between us not even I can explain."

"That doesn't make it right."

A gust of wind blew in from the south, and thunder struck over our heads.

"How do you know unless you give us a chance?" His other hand tucked a wayward strand of hair behind my ear, and I shuddered. His body pressed into mine. "I don't know why you insist on resisting this."

This being the irrational feelings between us. He was wearing me down. I no longer seemed to remember why I was fighting so hard against what he made me feel. It was exhausting working each day to stay away from him, to not give in to the urge to wrap my arms around him or kiss him brainless in the middle of math class.

He was a distraction.

And there it was. The reason Torent was bad for my health. If I spent all day staring at his gorgeous face, I'd fail all my classes. I'd be stuck in Havenwood Falls with Brooklyn breathing fire down my neck. I'd probably run off and marry him straight out of high school and end up with a dozen equally gorgeous little demon babies.

Sparks lingered at the places his fingers had touched my cheek. Torent, being part demon, could produce a light he called hellfire. I hadn't seen its full potential, but the bits I'd been exposed to were mesmerizing.

"You make me lose myself," I admitted softly.

His focus was completely on me, which was more than a little unnerving. "Why do you see that as a negative thing?"

I angled my face closer to his as if compelled. "I have dreams, plans for my future."

"It doesn't have to be one or the other," he said softly.

Maybe not, but I was afraid of how much I would be willing to give up for him if I let myself, because I knew with certainty that I would fall head over heels in love with him.

This conversation was getting too deep. It was time to divert. "Don't tell me you need a ride. Again."

Torent had used every creative excuse and then some to find time alone with me. It was impossible to not be flattered by his ingenuity . . . or his lingering looks and charming smile.

He gave me a lopsided grin. "The Jeep is in the shop."

"Uh-huh. You need to come up with new material."

His shoulders lifted in a shrug. "Why? This one works so well."

"Get in," I grumbled. I was going to regret this.

He lingered, keeping me pinned to the car with his body. "We're not done talking about you and me. Not by a long shot."

Strolling to the other side of the car, he opened the passenger door.

I exhaled the breath I'd been holding and slid into the driver's seat as he folded himself into my compact vehicle. He made it seem tiny.

Lifting his glorious tush up to one side, he pulled out my brush. "Is this yours?"

I winced, taking the hairbrush he dangled in the air. "Sorry. It was a hectic morning."

Torent relaxed back into the seat. "I heard you were late again."

I tossed the brush into the back of the car and stuck the keys into the ignition, waiting for it to kick over. "Are you keeping tabs on me, Stark?"

His lips twitched as he buckled his seatbelt. "I wouldn't dream of it."

I shifted the car into reverse. "Liar."

He leaned over the center console, fumbling with the radio as I pulled out of the parking spot.

"Are you going to tell me what has you on edge today?" He sounded like he was asking about the weather. "Or am I going to have to seduce it out of you?"

I smacked at the hand that had landed on my thigh. "Don't you dare. I'm driving. Do you really want me to get into an accident?"

He looked so adorable with his jet-black hair disheveled from the wind. "What I want is for you to admit you're enamored by me."

My mouth dropped open. The gall of him! Snapping my mouth shut, I put the Malibu into drive.

"Or . . . you can tell me what's going on," he prodded, as he was so good at doing.

I maneuvered my car in line behind the mass of vehicles trying to exit the parking lot, the weather delaying traffic more than usual. Someone's ball cap flew over the hood of my car and out to the field. I sighed, biting on my lower lip. What could it hurt to tell him the crazy conspiracy theories? It was likely I was worried for nothing. And the worst that would happen was Torent would laugh or tell me I was being silly. I could handle both.

"Beck is convinced I'm cursed. I think Brooklyn is still trying to get revenge on me."

Torent waved at Seth Cooper crossing the parking lot before his eyes ran over me. "Why would you think that? Has something happened?" When I didn't immediately respond, a glint of ominous suspicion sprang into his eyes. "Mallory," he growled so low it caused goose bumps on my arms.

"Geez. Don't get all demon on me. I'm sure it was nothing. I found a bunch of dead birds outside my window this morning."

His fingers brushed at the tiny stubbles under his chin that I found so appealing. The shadow of hair gave him an air of darkness I was clearly attracted to. "Why didn't you tell me?"

Shrugging, I flipped the wheel hand over hand, moving with traffic onto the main road. "I didn't think it was a big deal, but you and Beck are starting to freak me out over it."

Not entirely true. I had already been upset by it this morning, but for some reason, I didn't want to appear weak or superstitious. I didn't want to be that girl who ran to a guy every time she had a problem. I wasn't a damsel in distress who needed to be saved. I had every intention of saving myself.

"Birds often don't die in mass suicides, not in Havenwood Falls."

"I'm learning nothing happens in this town without a reason. I swear, if Brooklyn is still tormenting me because she blames me for taking her powers, I'm going to staple her ass to a chair." The thing was, with my abilities, I could very well carry out the threat.

The muscle along his jaw worked. "Let me talk to her."

"No!" I shouted, nearly swerving off the road. "Don't do that. It would only make things worse. I can deal with her on my own terms."

Torent scowled, either at my driving or at my refusal of his help. "Do you remember what happened the last time you faced off with Brooklyn?"

Did I ever. She nearly killed me. "How could I forget?"

"All the more reason you need to let me find out if she's behind this," he insisted.

"Do you think that's a good idea? You know how touchy she is about us. I don't want to push her and have crap escalating."

"So you're saying there is an *us*?" Torent's eyes twinkled.

How did our conversations always derail so quickly? It was an impressive skill. My lips formed a straight line. "Focus. We were talking about Brooklyn."

Some of the humor dried up, and he got serious. "Go out with me on Saturday."

Oh, my God. I give up. I was done fighting him. "Why would I do that?"

He leaned closer, and his fingers twirled a strand of my hair. "Because it would be fun. You remember fun, don't you, Mal?"

Okay, so Torent wasn't the only one with creative excuses. Mine just happened to always revolve around me studying or doing homework. But he had a point. I hadn't gone out in weeks, not even for coffee, and that was just a sin in my book. Locking myself up in the house was not me—it wasn't how I wanted to live. "If I say yes, will you stop asking? One date and that's it."

His lips twitched into a half smile. "One is all it will take."

I shook my head, trying to keep my eyes on the road.

"You really need to work on your confidence," I said dryly. The sky chose that moment to open up, letting the icy rain pour. It plummeted from the black clouds, hitting my windshield with a pattering force that made visibility dodgy. "What is this, the apocalypse?" I'd lived in Wisconsin. I was no stranger to winter, but this was nasty to the tenth degree.

"Maybe we should pull over until the storm passes?" Torent suggested, his eyes narrowing at the ominous clouds above us.

My fingers clenched on the steering wheel. "If I didn't know better, I'd swear you planned this."

He chuckled. "Controlling the weather is unfortunately not one of my skill sets."

I was slowly inching the car along the road and was seriously considering pulling over as Torent had advised. "But you have friends—"

What the hell?

A dark shadow was sailing straight at me, and I had no time to react, only brace myself for impact.

Whack!

I gave a yelp, my heart roaring in my ears. Something had hit the windshield. I stomped on my brakes, hitting a patch of black ice, and my car spun in a circle. Talk about déjà-freaking-vu.

Purchase *Ascending Darkness* where books are sold.

www.ingramcontent.com/pod-product-compliance
Lightning Source LLC
Chambersburg PA
CBHW052011170626
46808CB00007B/2878